REDEMPTION DAYS
by Andrew John Reed

Reserved literary property

© 2021 - 2024

Dedicated to my nephew Diego

Andrew John Reed

Redemption days

Another evening of work was coming to an end.

I couldn't wait to get home, relax in front of the television and have a cold glass of beer. My wife was visiting her parents and wouldn't be back for another ten days or so.

At that point, the idea popped into my head to organize a trip out of town with some friends. It wasn't a bad idea at all. I wouldn't have been denied a few days off, given all the overtime I had worked. So much overtime that, with the new course of cuts due to a sharp drop in income, I would have been paid half as much. So I had every right to ask for a few days off.

My bastard superior had been harassing me like a slave driver. He didn't like anything I did, he always had something to say. Asshole from birth! When I think of all the years I wasted on books, preparing for exams at university... and for what? To be under the classic daddy's boy. My blood boiled! Not to mention that he was much younger than me. When I was about to graduate, the brat was already sitting next to his father in the control room. Their caring parent had paved the way for him from the very first years of his studies, even going so far as buy him a degree so that he would not be disgraced. The family's good name had been saved even then.

After two years of working there, under the direction of the boy, the opportunity arose for me to escape and set sail for the new world. The company was also expanding into the United States. So I immediately requested a transfer, which was accepted by the management. My wife had been born there, so there would be no quarrels or arguments about the change, and she was even happy to return to her home country. She liked Germany very much, she was very happy there, but you can't rule your heart. She had always had the desire to return to the other side of the ocean. I was leaving my family, but planes were invented for long and fast crossings, so no problem.

The office was opened in New York, a chaotic city full of life.

Redemption days

The first years were quite traumatic, especially for me. Berlin was an international metropolis, but compared to New York it was quite provincial. The first flat we moved into was small but comfortable. We didn't need a lot of space because our pockets couldn't make much money at the time. I was the only one working, my wife was still looking for a job at the university or as an English-German interpreter and managed to find one almost five months after we moved in. That day, I took her out to dinner, at the most expensive restaurant in town.

After some time and a few more sacrifices, we finally bought our current house, a beautiful three-bedroom, two-bathroom flat with panoramic verandas, a kitchen, dining room, and a living room for my ultra-flat, three-dimensional big screen. A little electronic gem, costing a whopping 4,500 bucks! It's okay to be a little crazy now and then. As we didn't have any children to look after, we could afford a few luxuries, the TV, as well as some exotic holidays. Last time we went to Mexico, for about two weeks. It was a dream holiday that we would repeat.

Everything was going well, but sometimes dreams are marred by storm clouds full of nightmares. After six years of peace in the workplace, the brat appeared. Ironically, I had fled Germany because of him, and now he was on top of me again in New York City. According to the rumors that circulated and were later confirmed, Daddy had sent him to us to get him away from bad company (alcohol, sex, and gambling) and to try to straighten him out. If he failed to get his head on straight, he would be excluded from his father's will and lose all inheritance rights, not to mention that he had already halved his financial resources. We were again supervised by him, but he in turn was supervised by a man trusted by his father, whose task was to guide him towards a correct view of the business and to report everything he did. A guard paid by the pound. Given who he had to keep under control, whatever the old tycoon gave him was never enough. It wasn't hell, but it wasn't heaven either. It was approaching purgatory.

Redemption days

I had obtained the days off, but now I had to get the answers from my fellow travelers. I had made a mental calculation of the participants, There were supposed to be six of us, including me, but in the end, only three managed to get away. It was the usual ones: John, Matt, and Jason. We were all married, Matt and me with no offspring and Jason with two beautiful children, a boy of ten and a girl of seven. John, for his part, had a seventeen-year-old son by his first wife and another on the way from his second. The happy event was still several months away, but John could not wait. Whenever he had the chance, he would talk about the new baby, always showing us his baby's ultrasound scan. We were all elated to be leaving, and John hit the jackpot again. When I suggested that we disappear for a week, I was overwhelmed by their questions: Where are we going? When are we leaving? The hotel? The cost? These were all legitimate questions, but I had not yet given any kind of answer. I had to think about it on the spot, and the first destination that came to mind was the city of San Francisco, in California. The others were slightly puzzled by this proposal, none of us had visited it yet, but they were expecting a different, more lively destination. Like Las Vegas, with its countless lights, luxury hotels, strippers, green tables, and rivers of alcohol. An ideal choice for four men momentarily alone. It was going to be a week of pure fun! Unfortunately, there were objections from John to this destination.

‹‹ Look, guys. I'm glad we're going on the trip, but I don't think Vegas is appropriate,›› he said.

‹‹ What are you rambling on about? That's a great idea!›› replied Matt, all excited about spending a week in the mecca of sin and gambling.

‹‹ Do you remember why I got divorced the first time?››

At that statement, we remembered the reason for our friend's divorce. Years ago, when he was still married to his first wife, John got into the gambling business. Unbeknownst to anyone else, he would go to Las Vegas to bet on the green tables and lose big money. In the beginning, he bet small amounts, but eventually, those amounts increased a lot, as well as the losses. When he couldn't go in person, he used underground betting and found himself spending many nights in bad places, playing (and losing) poker. In the space of not even three years, he found himself on the breadline and without a family. Not even when creditors knocked on his door to seize all their few possessions he was able to stop playing, but at that point his wife asked him for a divorce, obtaining custody of their son. The judge forced him into a forced hospitalization in a clinic specializing in the recovery of chronic gamblers, and until he was cured he would not have the right to see the child. His wife suddenly found herself without any money, since he could not pay her alimony. Fortunately, her parents intervened, welcoming their daughter and granddaughter into their home and finding her a job to start a new life, far from her debauched and dangerous husband. John stayed about a year in that clinic. He came out completely rehabilitated, but without an occupation or a penny. His ordeal was not yet over. He got by with underpaid odd jobs until luck remembered him and his whole life took a downward turn. He managed to get hired by a large company and little by little he was also able to repay his alimony, both past, and future.

Redemption days

He tried to mend the relationship with his son, always under the watchful eye of his mother and his relatives, after all, he was the cause of the many sufferings and deprivations suffered by the boy and that was his last chance to make a breach in his son's heart. In the end, he managed to win him back and a new relationship was born between the two, stronger than the previous one. The most expressive change occurred when he met Mary, his current wife. From that moment on, his life stabilized forever. No headshots and not even a play at the lottery. He had changed his life. Every morning he went to church to listen to the services, and now and then he also gave his contribution to the religious community with some work. The change was radical. He had every reason to hate that place, and we apologized for our lack of respect for him.

‹‹ Excuse us,›› I said, giving him a consoling pat on the back. Then I resumed my speech.
‹‹ Better not tempt fate, not to mention that Mary would have killed you first. Your wife has a not bad temper!››

We laughed with gusto. Slightly bitter taste, though. The decision had been made. San Francisco. None of the others had racked their brains to find other destinations anyway, so we were going to spend a week of healthy fun in the city of The Rock!
Bookings were made through the internet, both for flights and accommodation, and it was decided to take a rental car, just in case we wanted to visit the surroundings of the city.

The hotel was only a few meters away from the nerve center of the metropolis. All the best nightclubs, restaurants, and sights were concentrated in that particular area of the city, so we avoided spending money on cabs. A walk certainly wouldn't have killed us, and then there was also public transportation, right? The weather was quite forgiving, not even a cloud would peep out for the duration of our stay, maybe too hot, that yes, but we certainly could not complain. Once we had unloaded our luggage in our respective rooms (John and me in room 245, Matt and Jason in room 247) and taken a nice invigorating shower, we went out to discover that wonderful city.

Near the entrance of the hotel, there was a small tourist information point, equipped with several brochures on places worth visiting. Matt and John, as soon as they saw it, threw themselves into it, looking for any useful information for our stay, and came out with about twenty folded publications in their hands.

‹‹ Wasn't one enough for you?›› Jason said, taking some pamphlets out of his hands to look at them more closely.

‹‹ You want to have fun, right?›› replied Mark, irritated.

‹‹ Sure, but we don't have a month, just a week.››

‹‹ Funny. I'm well aware of that. So we start with a visit to The Rock, then we'll see about the rest.››

We took the seats inside our compact car and, with its magnificent state-of-the-art satellite navigation system, we managed to reach the bay without any hiccups. The ferry was still moored at pier 41 and would shortly be leaving.

Redemption days

The crossing was fairly uneventful. The wind broke the entire bay with its strong gusts. Stupidly, I hadn't brought a heavy jacket or even a sweatshirt to protect me from that damn wind. Patience, I said to myself. There were about thirty passengers on the ferry, almost all tourists. I noticed few compatriots, the majority were foreigners visiting our country. Once ashore, a guide approached us, sporting his impeccable uniform and his customary '32-tooth' smile.

‹‹ Hello to you all, gentlemen. Welcome to Alcatraz, a place you will hardly ever leave!››

An impressive presentation, but not very convincing. I noticed that the other guides were making the same speech to the other tourists. So much for originality!

The visit began and Matt started reading the guidebook he had bought at the pier. According to all of us, his was a real mania. Every place he went, he had to get every kind of guidebook he could think of, even the most useless ones. He bought them anyway.

In the meantime, the real guide enunciated the curiosities of the prison. Matt nodded at him every statement, as if he were an expert on the history of the place, for years spent researching the area and not for simply having read something a few minutes earlier in his mini-guides. Jason wouldn't stop photographing every inch of the building. Even a withered and bare old tree at the entrance to the prison had the honor of being immortalized by his lens. We looked like a school group on a school visit, rather than adults on a field trip. Even with our respective families, we didn't have that kind of fun.

The visit was proceeding well. Matt kept us informed (maybe a little too much) about the history of the jail, repeating the guide's description word for word.

‹‹ Did you know that until the mid-1800s it was used for the protection of the bay?››

‹‹ We heard that too...›› replied Jason, as he set about to photograph yet another cell interior.

‹‹ Did you know that the prison is divided into four arms, independent of each other? In 1860 the fortress was built, then in 1907, it was turned into a military prison and only in 1936 into a federal one.››

‹‹ We know, Matt. Could you take your nose off those papers and be quiet for a few minutes?››

‹‹ I'm just trying to give you more information and... don't fuck with me John!›› and he walked away from the group with his guidebook clutched tightly in his hands.

The tour continued at the prison yard. Its high walls gave a strange feeling. Now I understood why it was considered the safest prison in the world. I couldn't resist the temptation and asked John to go back to the cell area.

‹‹ Why did we go back?››

‹‹ You should take a picture of me.››

‹‹ Don't tell me... You want to have your picture taken in the slammer, don't you?››

‹‹ I won't tell you, then.››

‹‹ But couldn't you have asked me first? Most people have had them taken.››

Redemption days

‹‹ I know, but I wanted to avoid that mess. So, will you take it for me?››

‹‹ What a disgrace!›› and laughed.

‹‹ Take it and don't make fun. Hurry up, come on,›› I urged him, stepping into an open cell and lying down in the jailbird bed.

‹‹ Try to get the whole cell,›› I recommended it to my official photographer.

‹‹ Shouldn't we call the others?››

He took the picture.

‹‹ We don't even know where they are,›› I said, getting up from the bed.

John handed me his digital camera and occupied my seat. He wanted the photo too. Once the photo was taken, he decided to change position. He opened the bars of the cell and put his arms out through the slits. Then he changed his mind. His eyes had seen an interesting object. The bathroom! A goliardic smile crossed his face and he headed for the toilet. He lowered his pants and stood over them in a thinking position, with a relative expression of great effort.

I snapped a couple of them and at that point it was I who occupied his place in the bathroom, to be photographed in that intense expression. Suddenly our two friends appeared and seeing me sitting in the bathroom with my pants down to my ankles, they couldn't help laughing. In the end, but, they too were photographed in that pose. At the end of the day, our inner child still lived inside us.

The visit to Alcatraz came to an end. We would be left with some nice photos as a souvenir.

That same evening we visited three nightclubs and realized that our metabolism was no longer what it used to be. We returned to our hotel rooms at one o'clock in the morning with our minds clouded by all the alcohol we had consumed. I didn't even change my clothes, not even after puking my soul out in the toilet. My dear friend held my head up, and I returned the favor, after not even ten minutes.

The rest was not peaceful, the head and the feeling of nausea did not leave me for the whole night. I vomited three more times before I was able to sleep. The next morning I felt the hangover and, considering the others, I wasn't the only one with a hangover.

The following days we used them to visit other interesting places and in the evening some local, but we contained ourselves in drinking. Two nights before leaving, I received a call from my wife.

‹‹ Hello dear, how are you?››

‹‹ All is well, thanks. You and the other big boys are having a good time?››

‹‹ We are all well and having a good time, yes. San Francisco is a beautiful city, we even managed to visit The Rock››.

‹‹ The Rock?›› he asked.

‹‹ Alcatraz. Listen, how are your parents?››

‹‹ They're fine too, they give you their regards.››

‹‹ Say hello back,›› even though I knew very well that his mother had never liked me.

‹‹ When are you coming back?››

‹‹ In two days, why?››

Redemption days

‹‹ Nothing. I'm calling you from the airport, I'm waiting to embark to return home. Work matters... so I'll come back early. Don't worry, I'll manage.››

‹‹ I'm sorry. I know how much you wanted to spend a few days with your parents. Come on, I'll see you when I get back. A kiss››.

‹‹ A kiss to you too and... say hello to the other lunatics in the group!››

‹‹ I'll tell them.››

We had dinner at an Italian restaurant in the Little Italy area.

The food was excellent and not even that expensive, and as a fitting end to the evening, we decided to pay a visit to the hottest club of the moment. And being in, we waited almost two hours to be able to sit at a table. The place in question was one of those themed ones, that sprung up a bit 'in every point of the country. As soon as you crossed the threshold, you were thrown back about sixty years, by the decor, the waiters' uniforms, and the type of courses. The prices, but, had curiously remained those of our era. Only Matt decided on a pitcher of beer, while we went for non-alcoholic drinks. Both the tables and barstools were occupied by patrons intent on every kind of alcohol and drink the house could offer. The respective phone calls, received from our wives, made us return to the harsh reality of our lives.

‹‹ I have to confess that I'm a little sorry to have to go home. How about you?›› said Matt, sipping his beer.

We nodded in unison. We didn't want to say that married life was boring or a prison, but sometimes we missed the single life, with all its fun and carefree youth. During my time at university in Berlin, there wasn't a day that I didn't get high with my fellow students. Drinking and smoking in the bathrooms and rooms of the university campus were a daily occurrence, as were all the women who passed under my sheets. Good times... Once I was married, all that had become just memories. Now I was content with a little poker night with my office colleagues and a few dates with them, but nothing more. The conversation had also changed a bit over time, and now we were talking more about family, work, and making ends meet at the end of the month.

At one point, Jason pointed to a table to our left. Intrigued, we turned in that direction and saw a disgusting scene. The table in question was occupied by two men, one of whom was dressed in a tight little shirt, earrings, and pants so tight that I wondered how he could walk. He could have been in his mid-twenties, while the other, more advanced in age, was wearing a designer suit, perhaps made to measure by an artisan tailor. All well-groomed and polished for the evening. So far nothing strange, but the gray-haired man had put his hand under the table and, thinking not to be noticed by anyone, he put it over the leg of his young friend. They both smiled.

John was the first to comment.

‹‹ Do you realize what those two are up to under the table?››
‹‹ He just put his hand on his leg... so what?›› replied Jason.

Redemption days

‹‹ Jason... look closer!›› said Matt, continuing to observe the developments of the scene, which was evolving in a certain direction. The elderly man became even more reckless. In fact, from his leg, he had advanced his hand until it stopped above the flap of his young companion. He was caressing him right on the penis, not caring that he was in a public place.

‹‹ Two dirty fags!›› said John, disgusted, turning away to avoid seeing that indecent contact. ‹‹ So what?›› echoed Jason, while he looked for the waitress to order another drink.
‹‹ So what? Are you going crazy? Those beings are sick, disgusting, and abnormal!›› I said with emphasis.

The others in the group agreed with me across the board, except for Jason's usual liberal. He would never change his mind. In other previous discussions, I had to restrain myself from grabbing him by the collar of his shirt and shaking him until he fainted, to try to get rational ideas into his big head. I cut the conversation short, to avoid unnecessary and inappropriate excitement, which would have ended the evening in an inelegant manner.
The other two patrons (the queens) paid their bill and left the place hand in hand as if everything was normal. At that sight, I turned around, so as not to let the blood rush to my brain from anger. How could such beings exist, depraved and against nature? I didn't know what to answer myself.

Jason had never understood how the world turned, and maybe he never would. More than once I would have liked to take him to one of the meetings of the association, so he could have opened his eyes to all the evil that plagued our world. Being a hard head, he wouldn't have changed his mind. But even though we were occasionally at each other's throats, he remained one of my best friends. Matt and John were on the same wave frequency as me. I eventually bet on them to join the association.

The evening ended like the night before, drunk to the point of vomiting the soul. By now, our excursion as singles in another State of the Union had come to an end. All we had left were the good memories and the big headaches caused by the hangovers. As Matt so aptly put it, "Once we returned to harsh reality, we would miss all that, and little by little the memories would become a blur."

When we returned home, we promised each other to plan another such trip, but we knew in our hearts that this would be our last. My wife, upon my return, told me about her parents and the work problem that had come up between her head and neck, which turned out to be quite complicated and important. The colleague who was in charge of that particular file had a minor car accident (not serious, she came out with a few broken bones) and had to be hospitalized. So, since my wife was the other executive in charge, she had to expect her return and take matters into her own hands in to save the company a few million dollars in damages. Fortunately, the deal went through, and to thank her, her superiors gave her a bonus of almost five hundred dollars. We celebrated with a dinner in the most luxurious restaurant in town, followed by a night of fire under the sheets.

Redemption days

One day we received an invitation to attend the birthday party of dear Clarisse, Jason's happy wife. It was a surprise party, held at their home and designed for a select few. Unfortunately, Clarisse's parents were unable to attend. They were elderly and lived in another state, so they decided to decline the invitation.

The party was put together at a reasonable cost, although Jason spared no expense when it came to his family.

As a distraction, Jason convinced Clarisse to go out to dinner, while the children would be watched by a babysitter. When they arrived at the chosen restaurant, he pretended to forget his wallet at home and backed out to return. Clarisse then suggested that she pay the restaurant bill herself. The heavens opened! Jason stated in a huff that the birthday girl could not pay for the birthday dinner out of her pocket, so the only solution was to retrieve the wallet. Back at home, Clarisse did not want to go downstairs to go with her husband. She would wait for him inside the car, so he would get moving, and no more precious time would be lost.

‹‹ Let's go together. I don't like you waiting here all alone,›› Jason told her.

‹‹ Don't waste any more time. Get in and retrieve your wallet››

‹‹ Don't you want to keep your hubby company?›› she pleaded.

‹‹ Jason, aren't you hiding something from me?››

‹‹ No, what would I be hiding from you? A mistress hiding in the closet? Come on, dear, don't be stupid.››

Jason had hit the nail on the head. Finally, Clarisse decided to go along with her husband's strange manias.

‹‹ All right, let's go get this damn wallet. Then it's off to the restaurant.››

When she opened the front door, the lights suddenly came on, illuminating a group of people who shouted in unison, "Surprise!" She was amazed and amused. Then she turned to her husband and hugged him in joy. She didn't know what to say. She thanked us one by one and showered kisses on her children, who were jumping from one side of the room to the other, throwing confetti and continuing to shout "surprise!" to their mother.

The chosen menu was almost all fish and white wine. Only the children are meat-based. Even the children, in their small way, had collaborated in the preparation of the surprise party, and Clarisse still couldn't understand how they had managed to keep their mouths shut all that time.

‹‹ Simple, my love. I have bribed them,›› replied her husband.

‹‹ What did your father promise you?››

‹‹ Dad promised that we could stay up like the grown-ups,›› resumed the youngest son with the serious tone of someone who knew better.

Redemption days

They both knew they wouldn't last past ten anyway. Serious children, diligent and respectful of adults, they had been brought up in the best of ways. Their mother cared a great deal about discipline and had raised them with a carrot and a stick since they were born, without ever raising her or Jason's hands against them. Corporal punishment was not part of their upbringing. Watching those little ones, my paternal sense peeped out, and for most of the year, it slept in the deep recesses of my subconscious. Fortunately, when it emerged, the spell soon vanished from my mind and I returned with my feet firmly planted in the ground, to my latest-generation LCD screen. At the end of the dinner, the main course made its entrance, the birthday cake with the inevitable song of good wishes and later delivery of gifts.

Once back home with a full belly, my wife Lorelain began to make the usual considerations about the party. On how it had been organized, on the dresses of the other guests, and other small considerations, which for me were more like gossip. The good thing was that she always wanted to involve me in her remarks and the end, I repeated to her what she wanted to hear, that is, her remarks. She kept talking from the bathroom, and finally, I said to her from the bedroom.

‹‹ Guess what they proposed to me in the office?››
She, in a slightly tired and sleepy voice, replied: ‹‹ Promotion and transfer to the German office››.

‹‹ Right! Won't you be a guesser?››
‹‹ I wish. Anyway, when can you refuse?››
‹‹ What do you mean?››

‹‹ In the sense that they're proposing it to you now, but eventually you might order it.››

I had not evaluated that circumstance, but there was no danger.

‹‹ Don't worry, they'll never do it. And then they'll get tired of asking me and eventually send someone else. Right now, though, I'd like you next to me, under this sheets.››
‹‹ Do you miss him much?››
‹‹ I've finished. Now let's all go to sleep.››

He slipped under the covers and fell asleep almost immediately.
I could feel her sweet, sensual breath on my neck, and I sincerely wanted to make love to her. Yet, tiredness had won the day, not to mention that the next day would be a busy one.

Redemption days

To make sure I didn't miss anything, the next morning I received a call from a member of the association, warning me of a meeting that same evening. I would again have to invent an excuse for my wife, who did not accept my membership in that particular association, and each time, there were endless discussions that led to furious arguments. I had also lost count of how many times she had asked me to leave her, and in the end, she had given up. Furthermore, I believed in their values, and nothing in the world would make me change my mind. So an unwritten compromise was reached. Every meeting amounted to an apology, even though I knew it didn't sit well with her, but that truce held well enough. I called her from the office to let her know that I was going to be home late that night and not to wait up. On the other end of the phone, I heard her just nod. The conversation ended there. Years later, for the sake of our marriage, we learned to nip that particular type of call in the bud. I went back to doing the usual paperwork until my departure time. I worked hard and tirelessly and finally made my way to the office. Furthermore, I arrived at my destination almost five minutes ahead of time, certain that I would find someone. I rang. Two short rings and a long one. A raspy voice asked me who I was. I answered with the password and the door swung open, letting me into the American Nation headquarters.

Our association was born in Alabama in the first half of the 1960s, and gradually our ideal of a more just world ruled by white men had gained followers in almost every State of the Union. Sometimes we joined other associations such as the American Nazi Party, the K.K.K., and my personal favorite, the Aryan Nation. But, we did not consider ourselves Neo-Nazis, none of us were Hitler supporters or swastika supporters, but our ideas were very like theirs. We believed that only the white race, once in power, could save the world from destruction, from the apocalypse engineered by the inferior races. No one realized what was happening to the backbone of any civilized and democratic nation. What dark plans lay behind those insipid associations of freedom, peace, and other such nonsense? How could they think of saving the world from the abyss with their ridiculous thoughts of brotherhood among peoples? How could we coexist with those inferior races who were ready to end us without fail? They wanted the destruction of the white supreme race! When I lived in Germany, I saw almost every day their devious takeover, worthy of the great Machiavelli. How many young whites were left without a job, without a roof over their heads, and without a crust of bread because of those inferiors who managed with their whining to steal their future? The great thing was that no one intervened to defend them, but when it came to the damned, you could see thousands of people taking to the streets in support of them. They were putting our shops out of business with unfair competition, then buying them back at bargain prices and increasing their power within our economy. This was a way of cleaning up their dirty money, which they had earned through illicit trafficking ranging from prostitution to drug trafficking. They were destroying them, and our hopes for the future, replacing them with their men, occupying key positions in the nation! In Germany, as in the rest of

Redemption days

the old continent, the so-called democratic rulers had taken the path of racial integration, protecting the inferior races at the expense of the chosen race. Those damn laws prevented the honest citizens like me to be able to express their disappointment freely, without being prosecuted on charges of racism. Something I hated!

When I arrived in the United States, I found a completely different world from the one I had grown up in. Here too, they were trying to integrate inferior races into the community, but the mentality was very different. I was spoilt for choice between various extreme right-wing political associations. Little by little, I delved into the political universe and looked at a few associations. I immediately discarded the K.K.K. because it only focused on a certain category of inferiors, but I intended to fight the greatest number of enemies. If we concentrated our forces in one direction, the other categories that threatened our race would have an easy time of it. Our weakness was precise that we were divided both in outlook and in battle. If we had been united from the beginning, those bastards would have been defeated long ago, I was sure of it.

After months, my choice fell on the American Nation. The name didn't say anything, it sounded like a cultural association or something, but when you read some of their pamphlets you could tell that it was a tough and capable association.

In 1986, a bomb was detonated at a Negro Baptist church in the state of Alabama, killing 23 people and injuring 80, some seriously. Some wounded died several days after the bombing, raising the death toll from 23 to 45. A much increase! In early 1990, the Federal Government completed its investigation and pointed its accusing finger at Richard Blatler, our mentor and founder of the American Nation. The newspapers of the time reported on the attack for several weeks, as did the local and national news, and then it was forgotten for several years until the arrest of our leader. The episode in question took place on a quiet Sunday morning. The summer sun was making itself felt even early in the morning, the summer would be sultry and dry. The church service had already started several minutes before, cars parked outside on the street, while some stragglers hurried into the building. No one had the slightest suspicion that there were three bombs inside the building, placed there the day before. At night, two men from the association broke in through the bell tower, which also served as the rectory, and broke open the door. They placed the three homemade devices at critical points in the building. The first, most powerful one was placed under the main altar, while the remaining two were placed under the right and left-hand counters.

Redemption days

At 10:35 a.m. a roar shook the entire neighborhood. Cars parked outside the church were badly damaged by the debris thrown out by the explosion. Some houses on the other side of the street suffered extensive damage, shattered windows, and rubble scattered dozens of meters away. The people of the neighborhood, after their initial bewilderment, poured into the street. The spectacle that came before their eyes was a real hell on earth. They came out in terror. They were screaming and calling for help from the people who had gathered in front of the scene of the tragedy. Two or three of them came out completely engulfed in flames, barely managing to walk a meter before collapsing in the middle of the road in excruciating pain. The first rescuers did their best to extinguish the flames that were engulfing them and gradually consuming their flesh. The bell tower on the right-hand side of the church turned into a giant torch. The bell at the top of the tower began to toll. A sad symphony. The fire brigade arrived within two minutes of the explosion, followed shortly by police cars and ambulances. Within half an hour, the area was closed to all civilians. No one was allowed in or out without the permission of the police chief, which was almost impossible to get. The few local police officers tried to keep the onlookers and journalists, who had descended on the animal carcasses like hyenas, at bay as much as possible. Photographers and reporters from all newspapers and television stations crowded around the yellow stripe in the vain hope of capturing with their flashes the moment that would bring them glory (and a lot of money).

In the meantime, other reinforcements arrived, including some FBI units, the only ones not wearing uniforms or any other clothing with their logo but who could be identified by their inquisitive attitude. Their presence meant that the investigation concerned the bombing section and not the common crimes section. The fire-fighting operations ended four hours after the explosion. Every effort was made to save the dozens of people still trapped inside the church, but unfortunately (not for everyone) the fire quickly destroyed the supporting pillars, causing the building to collapse and killing the people still trapped inside the burning womb. Two firefighters and seven blacks died in the collapse. "RACIST BOMBING!" It was one of many headlines that appeared in various editions at the time. The United States Attorney General gave an interview during a press conference to affirm their will to put the material perpetrators, and especially the masterminds, behind bars. The flags were flown at half-mast as a sign of national mourning, while all the political dignitaries attended the funeral of those African monkeys.

The preliminary investigations focused on the variegated galaxy of extreme right-wing associations. Little by little, some associations were discarded, until they reached the so-called triad, to which the American Nation belonged (with full rights). At this point, many of our followers felt the fetid breath of the authorities approaching, and the more cowardly ones chose to flee, denying their membership in the association, while the more devout ones resisted and remained to fight in the ranks of the American Nation. The car used for the operation (obviously stolen earlier) was abandoned in an isolated place, camouflaged as well as possible while waiting for it to be set on fire. That was a carelessness that we paid dearly for.

Redemption days

Two weeks later, two agents found the car and after some forensic analysis, some fingerprints, and gunpowder residues were found, which had been used to make the bombs. The feds were able to trace the buyers back to a construction company linked to our association. On a Tuesday morning, some 20 plain-clothed federal agents appeared in front of our headquarters with a search warrant in their hands, but there were only two members in the office that day, who were examining the new membership applications that were to be discussed later in the higher council. When one of them went through the usual ritual of recognizing members and instead of the password heard the words 'Federal Agents of the United States Government, he was unmoved and raised the alarm, he said, although many suspected that he had shat his pants in fear! The call with the chief brought no news, but he ordered them to come in and look for whatever they wanted, right down to the foundations of the building. We had nothing to hide and nothing to fear. He concluded by saying to avoid any kind of bullshit and that he would arrive at the headquarters immediately to check on the federals. Finally, the latter began their search. They were divided into groups of two. Some took care of the filing cabinets, others the accounting and mail books. They left political propaganda for last, including the leaflets we distributed for recruitment. Everything had to be screened by the authorities. If there were any clues, they would come out at once, and the handcuffs would be snapped, so the feds thought, but for the moment, nothing compromising was found.

About half an hour after the call, the chief appeared, accompanied by his closest lieutenants, and he was immediately met by the two members, who were worried about what had happened. He calmed them down across the board with a few "reassuring" words and then, leaving them with his lieutenants, headed for the one he believed to be in charge of the operation. He politely introduced himself to the uncouth individual: a below-average man, with an olive complexion, raven hair, black eyes, and a dirty Jew's big nose. He was wearing a dark blue suit with a light-colored mackintosh over it, new and well-kept, and the cut of which showed that it must have cost a lot. You could tell a mile off that he was one of them, our sworn enemy. Despite himself, the boss tried to be persuasive with this inferior and asked for explanations about what was happening inside his office, but he waved a piece of paper in front of his face (a warrant signed by a federal judge) which gave him the power to ransack the place. All in order, said the rough man, as he placed the damn piece of paper safely in the inside pocket of his expensive mackintosh. Our boss cashed in casually and smiled through gritted teeth. He knew he couldn't stand in their way... but... he wanted to know the reason for the repression, even if he knew it.

‹‹ You should know,›› said the rough man.

‹‹ What should I know?››

‹‹ Aren't you the head of this den of racists?›› he said defiantly.

‹‹ We are an association that sets itself the task of saving the white race... ›› clenched his fists in anger ‹‹ but you can see that you do not understand the real situation of the country since it has been on the rotten side of the country since its birth World!››

Redemption days

‹‹ Don't abuse my kindness. Don't leave town, we'll have to ask you some more questions.››

‹‹ I don't think so... but don't abuse my good nature either.››

The uncouth man left him alone in the middle of the room without even saying goodbye. Once he had left, our people arrived and surrounded the chief, creating a human barrier around him, to get some information about the situation. They decided to move to a secluded spot, as far away from prying eyes and ears as they could get in all that federal hubbub. They talked for a few minutes, taking stock of the situation, but were abruptly interrupted by the rough man and his henchmen.

What happened in those minutes is confusing: versions differed from each other. Members of both factions claimed to have been attacked by the opposing side. According to the coarse federalist's version, there was a strong and violent reaction on the part of our people to the arrest of the leader by the authorities, who were forced to engage in a furious physical fight, which ended with a few shots in the air to calm the spirits. The association's version completely turned the tables, as our leader was in the process of handing himself over to the authorities who had served him with the arrest order, but the uncouth officer got carried away and punched a member of the association in the stomach who had approached the leader to ensure that his constitutional rights were respected, at which point a fight broke out between the two factions, with gunfire. In the end, the report mentioned resisting arrest and insulting a public official.

They were all arrested and locked up in separate cells, which (according to the feds) meant that they were unable to communicate with each other to organize a common line, so they blatantly contradicted each other and so could be charged. The chief's interrogation lasted several hours.

No breaks.

The agents took turns, but the rough man remained present throughout the interrogation, without exposing himself personally. He remained behind the scenes as an observer. The chief's face showed no sign of relenting, cold as marble. He answered every question calmly and in a serious tone, always remaining vague and entrenched behind "I don't remember". The boss's superior attitude was paying off, as the agents were proving inconclusive with their questions. Finally, they decided to change their tactics and play them off against each other. The desperation cards. A move that did not bear the desired fruit, the loyalty of the members of the American Nation, could not be undermined by anyone, least of all the filthy federals. So they resumed with the direct questions: « We know that you are behind the attack. Confess and you will feel lighter».

« If you are so sure... show me the evidence »

« Do you think this is a farce? What are we climbing on the mirrors? Answer » the federal was no longer so sure of his plan.

« It's a statement from him, not mine ».

Redemption days

At that point, the rude, also called 'filthy Jew', motioned for his collaborators to leave, so that only the two of them remained inside the interrogation room. He and the boss were about to play the final game. One of the three went back in for just a second, left a canary yellow folder on the table, and left the scene again. The two were studying each other carefully, the torturer took a pack of cigarettes from his inside pocket, took one, and then made the gesture of offering one to the other man, but he politely refused: ‹‹ No, thanks!››

He would never accept anything from a cursed Jew. The rude nodded and left the packet in plain sight on the table and lit his damned cigarette. He took a few puffs. The dossier was still there, tightly closed. And now and then that homunculus drummed his fingers on the file, just to make a scene. They looked straight in the eye! They continued to study each other. The acrid smoke from the cigarette had invaded the entire room in a few minutes, but that bastard didn't care: on the contrary, as soon as he put out that one he lit another one. He hoped to annoy him with smoking, deluded. In the end, he said: "Did you want proof? Here you are! ›› and handed him the file. Our mentor took it in his hands and opened it, then began to read it carefully. The folder consisted of interrogation reports, wiretaps, and photos of various stalking carried out days after the attack. As he leafed through those pages, he began to understand that the bastards had found more than he thought. They had also arrested the three perpetrators of the massacre. He quickly read their confessions, where names, places, dates, and the location of the explosive devices appeared, and in some places, his name appeared even if there was not enough evidence that linked him to the massacre. In the home of one of the three weapons, balaclavas and some bags of explosives were found, all indications of guilt.

‹‹ Did the cat eat your tongue? ››

He closed the file and returned it to the sender.

‹‹ Surprised, isn't he?››

‹‹ Is this all you have in your hands? ››

Redemption days

‹‹ Just enough to make you rot in your homeland prisons for your whole miserable life ››

‹‹ This is only circumstantial evidence... it does not prove my involvement ››

‹‹ This is what you think... but the confessions of your subordinates speak for themselves... ›› he lit yet another cigarette then: ‹‹ This tough attitude will certainly not save you from prison! ››

‹‹ So you want to negotiate?›› said the chief in a superior tone. He understood their game.

‹‹ One hand washes the other, right?››

The coarse fed was not so surprised by the boss's attitude, he knew who he was dealing with, after all, it was not the usual extreme right-wing nutcase, he was a leader. He had single-highhandedly built a real subversive association that was able to concentrate many militants within itself, while at the same time managing to control the hotheads. The Federals made an extreme attempt to transform him into a first-class informer, but their efforts failed. They took him back to his four-by-four-meter cell with a bed, a sink (filthy and crooked), and a toilet for his bodily needs. They had him under surveillance by an officer who couldn't take his eyes off him and for safety's sake they even took the laces from his shoes, those bastards were afraid of his suicide. Ridiculous! Furthermore, they could hold him for 48 hours at the most, then without a valid charge they would have to release him and time was running out. Suddenly, the order came to release him: his lawyers had managed to get all those ridiculous and flimsy charges dropped, and the feds could not object. The boss greeted the uncouth man with a toothy smile and left the prison in the company of his lawyers.

On the evening of his release, he decided to organize a restricted and extraordinary meeting of the organization to take possible countermeasures and study new methods of fighting. No one could afford any more missteps, in which case it would be the end of them. The summit split into two distinct factions. One side considered the line they had taken to be the most effective and advocated its continuation, while the other faction intended to suspend any kind of sensational action until the situation had calmed down. Unfortunately, they were not only fighting over the line to be followed but also for the command post of the whole association. Alan Sernion, a slobbering old man, railed against the leader, accusing him of carelessness and inability to manage the demonstration action.

‹‹ You idiot! You trusted those three assholes! That job should have been done by real professionals! Fool!›› he said, banging his fists violently on the table. The boss remained silent. He stared at him coldly. The loyalists rushed to his aid and pounced on the traitor. At that point, a furious fight broke out. Three other men stood between him and the leader's followers. Insults and shouting were rife. To prevent the meeting from degenerating, the leader decided to suspend it. It was clear to all of them that the battle for power had just begun, but no one expected it to end quickly. Not even ten days later, the rebel faction, led by Alan Serion, left the association for good, in turn creating a new armed phalanx for Aryan power.

Redemption days

The much-feared split had taken place, causing a slight hemorrhage within the organization. The surviving council, almost decimated by the split, somehow tried to pick itself up and find a solution to end, or at best downsize, the new society born of that internal fracture. All those present were in such a state of agitation that each one tried to overpower the others with his voice to make his point. No one understood what the others were saying, and in the end, only one voice succeeded in calming them down: ‹‹ Gentlemen, please!››. Everyone was stunned and realized that their behavior had gone beyond the limits of decency. The meeting was able to start: ‹‹ Gentlemen, I know very well that the situation in which we find ourselves now is gloomy. The betrayal and the split have dealt us a heavy blow and, as if that were not enough, the federals have also got involved,›› he was interrupted by a murmur of disapproval. ‹‹ Rest assured that we will get back the place we deserve, and curiously enough, it will be the federals who will make us win it back››.

Everyone was amazed. Are the federals helping us defeat the traitors? Impossible! Some people turned up their noses and perhaps thought the boss had gone mad, but: ‹‹ My plan is as simple and workable as taking a sip of freshwater from a fountain. My assistant will now hand you a memo, where you can read a summary of the plan, which will be destroyed after you all have seen it for obvious security reasons.››

They had a quick look at the folder but finally asked the boss to explain the contents. The meeting ended after five hours of intensive explanations, questions, and discussions, followed by some consideration of possible weaknesses. In the end, everyone left the room with a relieved heart and a taste for revenge.

A month later, both the print media and the television stations were full of reports of a breakthrough by the authorities in the investigation of the massacre at the Alabama Baptist Church. After a long time, the perpetrators were brought to justice and sentenced for their crimes. Alan Sernion and close followers were arrested at their headquarters during a meeting of the association on charges of the racially motivated massacre. Eventually, our antagonists were put out of action by our sworn enemies, the federals. The Master's plan had yielded the desired results. At the end of the day, the feds and public opinion wanted a guilty party, and we had given them one. A victory on all fronts. We concentrated on individual attacks or small acts of intimidation on various civil rights associations and the homosexual community.

Two weeks later, I became a full member of the American Nation.

One morning, while I was absorbed in my office paperwork, I heard a definite knock at the door: a little annoyed by this intrusion, I invited the nuisance to come in. The door opened and my head of department appeared in his impeccable overgrew suit, accompanied by his classic smile for the big occasions that usually meant trouble for me. The last time, I had to work three weekends in a row without overtime, all because of a mistake on his part. As usual, I gave my customary smile.

Redemption days

‹‹ Have a seat, Ruben. Any news?››

‹‹ Yes, and it concerns you personally.››

He closed the door behind him and sat down unceremoniously in his chair. 'More trouble ahead', I thought.

‹‹ Tell me everything.››

‹‹ As you know, our company is working hard to find new staff to join our workforce,›› I nodded my head, ‹‹ the first selection was successful and out of the ten candidates, only two who fit our evaluation criteria remained. Two young graduates, ready to do anything to enter the ruthless world of multinationals.››

‹‹ Well?››

‹‹ You have been promoted to tutor.››

‹‹ Tutor? Are you kidding me?›› and I laughed.

‹‹ Listen to me before you laugh and say no.››

‹‹ I'm listening.››

‹‹ Your job will be to follow and guide one of the two young people chosen, not to mention that you can give him the job so to speak "unpleasant", plus your paycheck will weigh more, say about 350 dollars for the duration of the internship››.

‹‹ Interesting. The duration?››

‹‹ Three months, part-time, and you'll have your own slave.››

It was a very fascinating proposition, also from an economic point of view. I gladly accepted. The next day at 8:30 a.m., the trainee or slave would come to my office, depending on your point of view.

At exactly 8.30 a.m. the trainee appeared before my eyes, waiting in his elegant suit (perhaps the only one) for permission to enter the room.

‹‹ Come in and have a seat.››

After the usual introductions, I read his file, which contained almost his entire life story. He was tall, his raven black hair contrasted sharply with the blue of his eyes, and he had a lean, well-groomed physique, as did his choice of clothes. A 22-year-old genius! That's who I was looking at. Graduated with honors, top of his class.

‹‹ From what I can read in your profile, Mr. Reid, I can assume that you will have no problem making your way into this company, and I warn you, it will not be a picnic,›› I said, putting down the papers about him and staring straight into his clear, almost ice-colored eyes.

‹‹ I've never shied away from a challenge, and I'll do anything to improve myself. ››

‹‹ I'm sure you will.››

Redemption days

The interview was interesting in every way. The rookie would not give me any trouble and would carry out all my instructions without a word. For the first two weeks, I made him work like a mule, giving him several jobs that I did not want to do. He relieved me of a lot of work, and every evening I went home more and more relaxed. The rookie did all the jobs perfectly, didn't say a word, and had even managed to make a few friends among his colleagues. A fantastic helper! One evening, I decided to go for a beer and as I passed his office I spotted him hunched over some paperwork, so I invited him to 'The Rose' for a drink. As always, the place was packed with all sorts of white-collar types, all there to discuss shit. As soon as we got inside, I ran over to the only free table, and it was only after I'd sat down that I realized the newbie was standing in the doorway. I motioned for him to join me and take a seat at the table, he still seemed embarrassed by the invitation.

‹‹ Sorry, too many people››.

‹‹ No problem, it happens to me sometimes, but...››

‹‹ But?››

‹‹ But no sir, OK?››

‹‹ OK, so where are the toilets in this bedlam of human beings?››

‹‹ Straight ahead, then first door on the left... what do you take?››

‹‹ A Cube Libre, please.''

Upon his return, I found his order along with the classic dry Martini for yours truly. The evening took shape after five Cube Libres for the young man and eight martinis for myself. The ice had melted, as had our defenses. The young man told his story, avoiding going into details about his private life. He was originally from another state, he came from a small town with few people and no entertainment. He left his family of origin (all church and work as he said) to escape from that hole and moved to New York where, between a job and the other, managed to make ends meet and pay for his studies. After all, he was a good guy.

‹‹ I guess it's time to go home,›› I said, taking a quick look at my watch. It was a good thing that before leaving the office I had warned her about my delay, otherwise, Lorelain wouldn't have let me get away with it. I paid the bill and called a cab, in those conditions we wouldn't get home even with all our goodwill. The first stop was my house, then before saying goodbye, I gave the driver almost 70 dollars to pay for both rides and as I got out, I heard a 'thank you, to which I responded with a wave of my hand. I staggered to the front door, and finally (I don't know how) found myself in my own home, next to my sweet and dear wife...who was holding my head over the toilet, while I puked my guts out! The lecture was only delayed for a few hours.

I made up for that miss with a dozen choice red roses, a giant box of liqueur chocolates (her favorite), and an invitation to lunch. Forgiven, I hadn't lost my touch. During the meal, we talked about my evening in the company of the rookie.

Redemption days

‹‹ I can see you've taken the boy's fate to heart.››

‹‹ He's a rare gem... He's a nice kid with a lot of desire to learn: he'll certainly have a career, and at his age that's rare. Not to mention that the other boy is not very bright. He will learn a lot from me›› and I laughed, while the waiter brought us the food we had ordered.

‹‹ Even as far as night raids go?››

‹‹ I thought you had forgiven me... with what this meal has cost me.››

‹‹ Only half forgiven. He got to you, should I be worried?›› The second course was served with a slight delay.

‹‹ Worry? And of what?››

‹‹ Of your betrayal...›› but he did not finish the sentence.

He froze in time. We spent the rest of lunch in silence. That insinuation of his, had broken the romantic enchantment of lunch, he thought he was funny, but he never had much of a sense of humor.

That same night, she made up for her insult with some healthy marital sex. Under the covers he understood his mistake... his moans as a woman in heat proved my state of virility, other than filthy queer. I was a complete man and not 'half a man'! After sex, I lay awake thinking about that damned line of my wife's, many doubts came to my mind and one question, 'What had made her think I had become a deviant?' I was dating James, but I was seeing other men among colleagues and friends, fuck! None of them were sick! I wasn't the type to hang out with certain riffraff, then if one of them had just walked up to yours truly, I would have been able to spot him and punch him in the face! In the end, I thought back to the sex I had just had and said to myself in the silence of the night, "A queer wouldn't get a hard-on!".

Urgent news from the American Nation. The big boss wanted to see us for an extraordinary meeting, scheduled within a day. I had to postpone the appointment with James, notified him by text message, and apologized to him for the package. One day I would invite him when some calm had returned. Everyone was present in the big room of the association, only he was missing. Usually, he was always on time, but that time he wasn't there when we entered. A good half hour went by, we were getting worried, but then he made his appearance: ‹‹ Gentlemen, sorry for the delay. Unfortunately, the city is bedlam, but, let's not waste any more time and start the meeting immediately››.

He placed on the table the large envelope he had brought with him. ‹‹ As you certainly know, we are trying to organize in our beloved city a worldwide event of unprecedented depravity and immorality!›› and opened the file. We knew it very well. The media did nothing but hammer us with that event, but none of us took the floor, it was up to him and him alone to speak. ‹‹ The other night, I spent it devising a plan and gathering information to be used for the final purpose. After careful consideration, I was able to devise a federal-proof plan, but I will defer to your judgment. Dick starts to distribute this papers››.

Dick did his duty, fast and precise as usual. I read those sheets with avidity and could see that the plan was simple and precise, but had some flaws.

Redemption days

The chief resumed his speech: ‹‹ My dear compatriots, now that you know what it is, we can begin to discuss it. Any remarks?›› he asked an assembly of silent and ashamed people. Almost all of us had drawn more or less the same conclusion: The plan was not foolproof! He continued to observe us with his inquiring eyes, in a vain search for someone willing to discuss, and finally, I decided to take the floor: ‹‹ I would like to speak if there is no one else before me››.

‹‹ Go ahead and speak, and don't worry, I don't see anyone else itching to do so››.

‹‹ Chief, I want to be honest with you and everyone else. I don't want to hide behind any catchphrases or turns of phrase, so I'm going to get right to the heart of the matter. On a first reading of the dossier, it is safe to say that the plan has some not insignificant flaws from a security standpoint. My idea would be to ally ourselves with the other associations closest to us and organize the demonstration as best we can, but in the meantime, all violent acts should be suspended››.

The buzz among my affiliates became louder and more open. I had triggered a bomb! They were accusing me of betraying the leader, just because I had dared to object to his plan. All those stares fixed on me. Cowardly and ridiculous looks from real professional ass-kissers. The boss remained silent, then: ‹‹ The meeting is over. I expected more courage from you, but I realize I was wrong. So I will give you a few days to study it all and propose changes. You can go... except you. You stay, I want to exchange a few words. Goodbye to all››.

I was petrified by that request. Perhaps I had overcome the invisible barrier that divided the supreme leader and his followers, or perhaps I was making the gallows alone?

Now we are alone, and we can talk in peace," and I was silent and motionless like a statue.

‹‹ You've been loyal, and I appreciate that. You didn't keep quiet like that bunch of sheep with their backsides too tight with fear››. Damn! I had broken through to the boss! A stroke to use to my advantage, I thought.
‹‹ What you said is right. My plan isn't perfect, but you've also sinned in naivety››.

He took a smuggled Cuban cigar from his jacket pocket and lit it naturally, without asking me if it bothered me or not. For my part, I pretended not to, even if the smell of smoke was making my eyes and throat burn. I smoked cigarettes, but I couldn't stand the secondhand smoke on my face.

‹‹ What would be my sin of naivety?››
‹‹ The union with the other associations is weak, and I believe that in that case there could be defections among our ranks and so-called raids... dangerous›› he sucked in the smoke from his cigar and immediately released it into the air.
‹‹ The rest of the plan might go, but I'm not entirely convinced yet.››
‹‹ Then what could we do?››

Redemption days

‹‹ Let's wait until the next meeting to hear the opinions of the other members, then we'll consider what to do.››

That interview ended with a vigorous handshake between me and the chief and my promotion to his right-hand man! I couldn't believe this unexpected promotion, so much so that I pinched my arm to convince myself that it wasn't all a dream.

Work was going well, my protégé was giving me a lot of satisfaction and I was happy for him. His internship was almost over (time was slipping away too quickly) when I received news from the top that James would become part of the big company family and that I would become his direct superior. At that news (which had not yet been communicated to him), I took the initiative to organize a dinner at my house to announce the happy event. Living alone in a big city, far from his family, he would have been pleased to celebrate his hiring in a warm and familiar environment, not to mention that it would have been the right occasion to introduce him to my wife. After getting the go-ahead from my better half for the dinner invitation, I went to his office to officially invite him.

I knocked and entered that small room, furnished with the essentials: a desk, metal shelves used as a bookcase, a picture hanging on the only free wall – a simple print depicting a night view of the city – and finally a large and bright window located behind his desk. I greeted him warmly and sat down in the chair in front of his desk.

‹‹ Hello. Finally, a familiar face. How are you?›› James said as soon as he caught a glimpse of me, smiling cheerfully but a little tired. I returned his greeting but seeing him so cheerful, I had the doubt that someone had already made him aware of his employment, so I decided to investigate.

I said: ‹‹ You're bubbly today, have you received any good news?››

‹‹ None in particular. This morning I got out of bed on the right foot, that's all.›› ‹‹ Any wishes?››

‹‹ Nothing work-related. I was wondering what your plans are for the day after tomorrow.››

‹‹ My plans for the day after tomorrow? I don't know why that question?››

‹‹ Simply because I wanted to invite you to dinner at my house, nothing pompous, a simple family dinner.››

‹‹ I thank you... let me think, let's say I have no commitments, so yes, I can accept your invitation though...››

Redemption days

The commander's voice, coming out of the loudspeakers and announcing the temperature and climate of the destination, roused me from that terrible drowsiness into which I had sunk in the vain hope of being able to rest, at least for a few minutes. In those damned minutes that preceded the landing phase, my mind was loaded with countless memories, old and new, in contrast to uncontrolled emotions that would soon explode like a river in flood. After an intercontinental flight, I found myself at Berlin International Airport in line for customs control, after which I took the first free cab and was taken to the suburbs. As I walked through the center of the capital, I noticed with amazement the great architectural changes that had taken place within it years after my departure for the United States. The various post-reunification governments had gone to great lengths to give the entire city a new look as if this would erase twenty years of the nation's history, and all to build a kind of social virginity in the eyes of other nations. Absurd! I paid 87 euro for the ride and got off in front of the entrance to my birthplace. Time had not discounted that little house made of red bricks and wood, not at all. After the death of my father, all the weight fell on the poor shoulders of my mother who, as long as she had the strength, tried to keep it in a decent state but eventually had to surrender to old age. The neighborhood had changed, and I must say for the worse, unfortunately. From a suburb for middle-class families, with time it had turned into an infamous one with a maximum concentration of immigrants of various ethnic groups, especially the Turks and blacks who eventually took over from the German families who disappeared little by little.

I stopped for a few seconds in front of the metal gate (consumed by the rust) breathing deeply the healthy air of my land and headed for the main entrance. I didn't even have time to put my finger on the doorbell when the door opened in front of me and, to my surprise, a well-groomed woman in her fifties appeared on the doorstep, dressed formally and greeting me in perfect German. She was a damn black woman! I couldn't believe that a woman of that inferior race was looking after my mother! I held back from giving her a good punch on that monkey face, I returned the greeting, I put my suitcases at the entrance of the house and without waiting I headed towards my mother's room, but she stopped me grabbing my arm: ‹‹ Pardon me, sir, but you have to wait a few minutes in the living room››

‹‹ Are you kidding me? I have to see... or rather I want to see my mother immediately and take your hands off me, do you understand?››

‹‹ Excuse me for being so familiar, but you have to wait. Take a seat in the armchair, then I'll call you... ››

‹‹ Do you realize who you're dealing with?››

‹‹ I know very well who you are, but your mother gave me strict orders about when you would arrive. So, take a seat in the living room and relax.››

‹‹ Do us both a favor and let me pass immediately!›› I ordered her raising my voice, I was losing my patience with that damned monkey, but she had not yet finished speaking with her shrill voice: ‹‹ I repeat that the lady must settle down before receiving you. These are her wishes, so please sit down››; at the end, I surrendered, I accepted those conditions and I retired to the living room waiting for her call. I sat down in an armchair and looked around. My mother had kept most of the old furniture, except for a small crystal table in the center of the room.

Redemption days

‹‹ Now you can come in, your mother is waiting for you.››

I couldn't remember how many years had passed since I had last seen her in person, but looking at her now, in that almost vegetative state, lying on the bed with all those electronic devices that helped her to live, my heart tightened. The darkness in which the room was immersed made the situation seem even more macabre. Now the woman who had raised me with an iron fist and so much love was nothing more than a shabby copy. I greeted her with a soft voice, while "that one" left us alone not without having reminded me (for the umpteenth time) to avoid strong emotions and not to tire her too much, as if I didn't know how to behave in certain situations. My mother looked at me with her clear eyes, dulled by the illness that was slowly bringing her to me. I noticed a chair next to the bed, I sat down and took her bony, wrinkled hand between mine. I squeezed it gently to let her know that I had finally reached her bedside, at which point she turned her head wearily toward me and tried to shake my hands.

She smiled.

A sad smile of death.

Her eyes saw nothing but darkness. She tried to talk to me through the oxygen mask, but I warned her not to tire herself out, so I began to tell her a little about my life during the years we had been apart. Tears ran down my face and my voice became less and less confident so that I had to stop to calm down. She followed my conversations with difficulty, trying with all her little remaining strength to remain alert. My mother, who had once been a strong and sweet woman at the same time, was abandoning me. The beeping of the device continued to echo in my brain, and I tried to drown it out with the words that came out of my mouth mechanically... until silence broke through that sad day: I was left alone.

Redemption days

In the following days, I took care of the paperwork and fired that woman. I later learned that it was my mother who had taken her on, as she was a trained nurse, and that it was she who made the call to alert me to her deteriorating health that damn night. Few relatives, whom I didn't even know I had or had lost contact with, attended the funeral. My mother did not put her wishes in writing, as she did not have much to leave. Not even the house was worth much and since I was the only heir I decided to sell it at a price below market value, including the furniture in the price. I took away only the personal effects such as family albums, old letters, and the few jewels she owned, the clothes I donated to the local parish, for the poor. I was sure she would have wanted it that way. Lorelain asked me how I was and if I needed help, offering to leave on the first available flight, but I refused, telling her that I wanted to be alone and that once I finished my task there, I would leave again. She fully understood my pain and my desire for solitude and said goodbye, reminding me that she loved me. It took me a week to resolve all the bureaucratic issues regarding my mother's death; the sale of the house would have taken longer, so I decided to donate it to the parish to make it a recreational center for the elderly of the neighborhood to be named in her memory.

I returned home and there, on the threshold of the apartment, I was embraced by my wife who began to cry for my mourning, although she reproached me for not having allowed her to reach me to help me and attend the funeral of her mother-in-law. When she fell asleep I got up and went to the living room, I took a bottle of whiskey from the liquor cabinet and I drank it all: I had to get drunk to forget. Tears streamed down my face again. My mind tried to remove the pain of my mother's disappearance but to no avail. Alcohol did not remove the ghosts of the past, the fears, and the regrets that had accumulated over the years of distance. Suddenly, I covered my face with my hands to stifle my crying when I saw her standing in front of the door.

‹‹ Let it out... come on, let it out...›› she said, approaching me and holding me close. A long hug and a liberating cry on her shoulder.

‹‹ It's okay now. I'm sorry, I didn't mean to wake you up.›› and resumed sobbing like a small child.

I wanted to hold back, a man should not cry, in front of a woman, but I could not stop.

‹‹ Let it out, go ahead, let all your tears out, come on››.

‹‹ I could have done more for her and I didn't!››

‹‹ Don't worry, you've been a good son, and you've never made her miss anything››.

‹‹ Unfortunately, I made her miss the most important thing, my presence. If I had moved to Germany or if I had never left, maybe I could have saved her... I would have stayed by her side... I would not have forgotten her!››

Redemption days

Lorelain ran her hand through my hair to reassure and calm me. Her hands caressed my face and at the same time gently wiped away my tears, I was devastated by the great loss.

‹‹ If we had the chance to go back and change some episodes of the past, we would never again be able to appreciate the memories of our loved ones. Don't take on guilt that you don't have... now come to sleep, you need it,›› so saying he helped me to get up from the sofa and took me to the bedroom.

The sleep was not the most peaceful, the fears, the doubts created real terrifying ghosts. At that point, I decided to throw myself headlong into work and the association's commitments, away like any other to forget my sorrows.

The weeks passed, and my pain diminished, but it would be years before I would stop suffering for good. One evening Lorelain suggested that we treat ourselves to a weekend away to relax, she already had in mind the place and the motel, where we would stay, a nice little place in the open countryside, and when she made me promise that for the duration of the stay, the phones would remain silent and that work problems and all other concerns would have to stay in town, I gladly accepted. A few days of complete relaxation would do us both good. After six and a half hours of travel, heading north on Highway 12 through open countryside and a few sporadic urban centers, we arrived in a village of not even a hundred houses, gathered around the main square with the most characteristic monument to the fallen of all wars. We passed the center of the village to take a secondary road, dusty and without asphalt, at the second fork, we took the junction on our right and finally reached our destination. I stopped the car in a dirt clearing, right in front of the main entrance of the building, and my first thought at that sight was: "A cough... and everything collapses on us here!".

Redemption days

The photos published on the website must have been several years old, but this did not change our minds about the weekend of rest. I unloaded the little luggage from the car, just in time to be received by the owner, a big woman of 220 pounds, dressed completely in black, who welcomed us to 'Maison Gold' and begged Karl to go out and get the guests' bags. The one who came out of that door and approached us to take our bags was not at all human: more than six feet tall, uncoordinated in his movements, dressed in a white T-shirt and olive green overalls, and with a face deformed by a hare lip, hands as big as shovels, he looked like a mental retard, because he expressed himself only with meaningless grunts. He took the suitcases, after having made an awkward bow, and carried them inside the Maison, under the watchful eye of the big woman and mine. In addition to the decadent appearance of the structure, there was also the deformed on duty.

The beginning was not the most promising. We found out later that Karl was the only son of Mrs. Olmert, owner and sole administrator of the B&B 'Maison Gold'. While the son, or whatever he was, carried our suitcases directly to our room, the lady offered us tea with freshly baked cookies and made us comfortable in the living room of the house. I had to admit... the interior was acceptable compared to the exterior. The furniture, although old-fashioned, was not bad, indeed it gave a touch of rustic, almost colonial to the whole environment that appeared comfortable, warm, and clean. The woman knew how to do both cleaning and preparing cookies, which I devoured almost all of. I complimented her on those chocolate-covered delights and took two to eat in our room. Both she and my wife crossed their eyes and smiled in delight to see a grown man regress to a childish state over homemade cookies. The room didn't disappoint, it matched the rest of the house, perhaps they could have changed the pattern of the wallpaper that over the years and exposure to sunlight had brought it closer to a brown, almost 'poo' but the rest was fine. Comfortable bed, clean, a large closet in finely carved wood, a desk, and a beautiful window that overlooked the main courtyard.

Redemption days

That evening at dinner in the dining room, the owner entertained us with some anecdotes about the house and served us delicious dishes just taken out of the oven. She had spared no effort in preparing them, also because the only guests were us, we were in a dead period. The table was set simply with plates of fine porcelain and crystal glasses, the only thing missing was the silverware to be at the level of a luxury restaurant, which the lady knew how to do. Baked meat, potatoes and salad, fruit, and a chocolate cake for dessert, all washed down with excellent Californian wine and just enough water. Mrs. Olmert did the honors, serving us personally.

‹‹ A weekend in this quiet place, how come? You look like a young couple... Excuse my curiosity›› she asked, while she cut a big piece of meat on her plate. ‹‹ No problem, we were simply looking for tranquility. Take a break from the noise and chaos of the big city,›› Lorelain replied amiably, casting a furtive glance at Karl, who was eating his dinner like a six-year-old who had just discovered the use of cutlery.

A child trapped in an adult body. The lady defined him with these loving words. Perhaps she had noticed my wife's interest and played along. Lorelain felt herself dying inside and tried to apologize for her unspeakable behavior, but the lady cut it short gently: ‹‹ Unfortunately, my Karl was born prematurely and this caused him to have learning delays. The doctors assured us that with proper care, he would be able to recover at least 70% of his functions. Every day for several years, my poor husband and I followed their directives down to the smallest detail and I can tell you that there were improvements, until that cursed day...››.

‹‹ Cur... sed d..d...day! Damn-it-all!›› suddenly screamed Karl, beating a series of blows on the table, so powerful that the glasses overturned and the cutlery and plates clinked. His eyes lit up with an evil and unnatural light at the same time, while his mouth deformed further, letting out a baritone and mournful grunt. At that point, his mother intervened and managed to calm him down with a simple caress of her hand and sweet words whispered in his ear.

‹‹ Excuse him, unfortunately, dramatic and painful memories of his mental state have resurfaced. I'm sorry, again... I'm so sorry for what happened.››
‹‹ We're the ones who have to ask you to help us.››
‹‹ We are the ones who should apologize, I should not have meddled in your life,›› Lorelain tried to apologize, feeling solely responsible for Karl's sudden reaction. The lady absolved her with a simple nod. At the end of the day, it wasn't any of our faults, maybe she should have avoided talking about it in front of her son. The dinner resumed slightly subdued, but there were no further incidents. In my thoughts, the possible conclusions of the evening took shape like in a black and white film, and they all ended with Lorelain's attack and my death, in a vain attempt to save her from the retarded humanoid. At the end of dinner, the lady invited us to take a walk in the moonlight.

Redemption days

During the walk, we came across an old barn a few meters from the house, and ... sex done on vacation is always the best! The next morning, around half past eight, someone knocked on our door firmly. We were still sleeping soundly, but that knock entered our heads, she turned away and mumbled something that meant: "Go see who breaks at dawn", so I got up to see the pain in the ass in the face, even though I knew who it was... in the whole house there were only four people and two were in this room, so... ‹‹ I'm coming, one second...›› I opened the door and here was the surprise: At my feet, I found a tray full of delicacies and treats for our breakfast in bed and the empty hallway. I thought it was the boy who had brought the tray, however, I picked it up and brought it to Lorelain, avoiding spilling anything on the sheets or the floor. We enjoyed our breakfast comfortably lying on the bed and I noticed with amazement that the lady had not forgotten her famous (for me) chocolate cookies that I devoured instantly. Once downstairs we thanked the lady for the trouble of having breakfast in the room, telling her that she shouldn't have, and she said: ‹‹ A small gesture to make me forgive last night's incident. Karl is no danger, he couldn't hurt a fly.››

Maybe it was so for her, but I thought that 'little' Karl could have killed another human being with unprecedented ferocity, and for sure in some time I would have read the news of his departure because of his son in the newspaper. I was sure of it. The morning was spent outdoors with a picnic basket and two bicycles as means of locomotion to reach an open space not far from the 'Maison Gold'. When we arrived at the place, we found other people who had the same idea as us, but most of them had come by car. Couples of boyfriends, groups of friends and married couples accompanied by their offspring were competing for that space, so as soon as we found a free place we sat down to taste the food prepared by Lorelain under the supervision of Mrs. Olmert. After eating, my wife took out a digital camera from her backpack and started to immortalize every inch of the clearing. It didn't matter if other people were in the frame, she would shoot and then go in search of new landscapes to photograph. A carefree smile lit up her face, I fell in love with her even more. Then she sat back down to enjoy her apple pie, I grabbed my camera and clicked! I snapped a sneaky picture, and she said, ‹‹ Damn... I wasn't posing. I'm sure it looked like crap, so let me see,›› she said, amused. I played with a few buttons on the camera and displayed the photo on the screen, which wasn't bad at all, on the contrary. Of course, she didn't agree and tried to take the camera out of my hands to erase it, but she gave up, underneath she liked it. Weekend ended.

Redemption days

We were returning home, calm and rested, at the end of the day everything had gone well, and we were already thinking of going back for about ten days. We met a few cars on the way back, we could have found a snag inside the villages, but it didn't matter, no one was chasing us, and we weren't in a hurry. At the time of the ceremony, the two women greeted each other with an affectionate embrace. Anyone who had witnessed that scene would have thought it was a greeting between two longtime friends, after all, Lorelain managed to win people over in a short time. In the car, I realized she had a few things to tell me, but I had to give her the 'L' to start.

‹‹ Tell me everything, come on.››

‹‹ Tell you what?››

‹‹ What you have to tell me is that you've been holding back since we left.››

‹‹ What makes you think that?››

‹‹ Your state of expectation, that's what.››

‹‹ State of expectation?›› and she turned to me, curious about that definition.

‹‹ When you want to tell me about some event, but you don't want to tell me about it, you get quiet and impatient... tell me everything.››

Then, finally, he told me about Karl: as soon as he was born he seemed a healthy child, the first doubts came after the fifth month of life, when the parents noticed the difficulties of their son remaining seated and the strange movements of the limbs like those of androids. The moments of alienation from the outside world became more and more frequent, then he isolated himself completely. At that point, they decided to take him to a pediatrician who, after a careful preliminary examination, had him urgently admitted to a specialized clinic to undergo more in-depth examinations. The little boy spent eight months in the hospital without the overnight presence of his parents, who were forced to make exhausting journeys of hope and take turns not to leave him alone. The doctors did all sorts of tests that debilitated the child even more. In the end, it was an external specialist who understood Karl's real situation: he discovered that the cause of his hell was a virus that caused a degenerative disease that in extreme cases led to the death of the patient but, if it was caught in time and if the proper therapies were administered, it left some chances of survival. Between the treatments and the various periods of hospitalization, the costs rose to the point that the health insurance refused to cover further expenses, forcing them to make a new life choice: they turned their house into a motel to earn money to cover medical expenses for their son. The treatment produced the desired results and the danger of death was averted, but unfortunately, the brain damage had compromised the natural development of his brain.

Redemption days

The years passed and Karl grew physically but not mentally, but his family didn't care, they just wanted him to be alive. One evening Karl, having seen an advertisement for a toy, began to scan the name of the product and every time he saw it on television he became euphoric, so his parents decided to please him, after all, it was not even an expensive toy, the object of desire was a radio-controlled car, bright red with rubber wheels for all types of tracks (so said the ad). On Saturday evening they decided to go all together to the nearest shopping center because it was in a dead period, and they thought that an outing would do them all good, but fate had other plans. Dark plans that would have indelibly marked their lives. After buying the toy and a tour of the stores, they made their way back home, but a group of thugs targeted Karl and a furious argument broke out between them and his father, which, thanks to the intervention of security agents, turned into a fight. The thugs were removed from the mall, while Karl and his parents headed for the parking lots, leaving the uncivilized act behind. Somehow the thugs, who in the meantime had called for reinforcements, managed to track them down and attack them: three of them blocked Karl, while the other four threw themselves at Victor, after having knocked down the lady who wouldn't stop screaming for help. Karl freed himself (he had the brain of a child but the body and the strength didn't) and ran in the direction of his father, who was on the ground and was trying in vain to repel the blows of his attackers. His face had turned into a painful blood-red mask, and the pain prevented him from screaming and reacting. The mother was in a state of shock and would not stop screaming. One of the attackers, alerted by the fleeing mongoloid, went towards him, and they got into a violent melee. The hooligan initially got the better of Karl until unexpectedly the tables were turned, and he took him by the throat with such force that he managed to lift him off the ground a few inches, throwing him to his right as if he were a dry branch. At this sight, the others interrupted their father's beating and threw themselves at Karl, who managed to put them to flight. Mrs. Olmert remembered nothing of that episode, only confused scenes and nothing else. Karl knelt next to his father's body and tenderly took his head, covered with blood, in his hands and started to sing the lullaby he always sang to him to make him fall asleep. The man died in his arms while a small crowd was gathering, together with the rescuers, to give them first aid. Lorelain ended the story by exclaiming, ‹‹ I want to have a baby!››

We arrived home.

After returning home I carefully avoided talking about the 'baby' even though I knew the day would come when I would have to face it.

Redemption days

The trouble came from the association because during my absence there were some intimidating raids in the so-called 'gay street' and against some civil-rights associations. Small isolated episodes. I understood that the news of my promotion had spread and some members must not have liked it and that they must have plotted to thwart me during my absence. In the course of an informal evening, the cursed ones showed off the front page of a local newspaper, where I read in big letters: "HELL AT DRAG QUEEN'S! Arson. 35 PEOPLE DEAD LOCKED INSIDE THE BURNING CLUB! Authorities are investigating racially motivated matrix!". They displayed it as if it were a drawing made by one of their children. I demanded an explanation about that intimidating gesture, also because I was supposed to be the one directing that kind of action and their answer was cutting: ‹‹ Since they couldn't trace you, they decided to go over your head and take action!›› said Michael 'Mouse-face'. How I hated that bastard!

‹‹ Very well, successful action, but I'd like to be warned before next time if it doesn't cause too much trouble››.

‹‹ Certainly...›› and smiled despite himself. Maybe they were expecting a rant from me or something, but they were disappointed, and I understood that "Rat Face" was the leader of the coalition that I would have to keep at bay and fight. He must not have been down with the choice of leader, because he had always coveted that position, and it was no mystery to anyone, given how he kissed his ass at every opportunity. I went into a room, I wanted a place where I could think quietly and rearrange my thoughts to prepare for the countermove. I lit a cigarette and... ‹‹ Smoking kills, don't you know that?››

‹‹ Fuck, guys... I disappear for a few days, and the first asshole on duty tries to kick my ass? Have a seat and give me a quick report.›› The boys came in and closed the door.

‹‹ What can I say? Michael just wanted to look good in front of the boss,›› John said.

‹‹ You too... couldn't you have warned me of the situation when we met at the market?››

‹‹ Excuse me, but you know very well what are the rules outside the association›› he justified himself, and he was right.

‹‹ None of us are to blame, the only culprit is Rat Face››

‹‹ All right, but the boss?››

‹‹ The boss?›› repeated Matt surprised.

‹‹ Yes, the boss... how did they get him to support this decision?››

‹‹ Simply by obtaining a majority of delegates, we opposed it, but it was useless.››

‹‹ That's fine, but...››

‹‹ You want to know why he didn't veto it, don't you?›› I nodded affirmatively,

‹‹ You know as well as I do that the old man is tired by now, not to mention that he is sifting through the candidates for the succession at the top of the association. He aims to ferry the transition smoothly, without fractures.››

Redemption days

Matt had a point, an internal war for power was brewing, and we would be part of it. At that moment I observed the eyes of my interlocutors and I saw the light. The light of power. The light of revenge. The light that illuminated our souls in moments of action. No discussion within the association, but we decided to meet at John's house for more security. The handshake between me and my friends sanctioned the beginning of my rise to power.

Unfortunately for me, the trouble was not over, it continued at home. As I was getting up from the table after dinner, she launched the attack: ‹‹ Mark, when you decide to address the topic?››

‹‹ What topic, sorry,›› I replied, playing dumb.

‹‹ You won't be able to run away forever, and eventually you'll have to face the issue, and the time has come!›› maybe for her, but not for me.

‹‹ I have never run away in front of anything, let alone for this reason›› she took the ball in her hands.

‹‹ Alright, now we sit down and talk››. I took my place at the table and with a friendly and serene tone, I told her that she could begin to discuss the situation.

‹‹ Mark, I'll tell you what I told you in the car on the way back from that weekend. I feel ready to have a child!››

‹‹ Excuse me Lorelain, but since we got married you have never mentioned your desire for motherhood. I wouldn't want it to have anything to do with that big woman's crazy son!››

‹‹ And here's one of your classic bloody answers!›› he was warming up.

‹‹ I didn't mean to be rude, so try to calm down! None of us are on trial!››

‹‹ Talking to Mrs. Olmert resurfaced a desire that had been dormant for years. After we got married, the desire to become parents was strong in both of us, and you know it too›› he was attacking, and his blows were low and well given.

‹‹ Time passes and people can change their minds or perspectives on the future!››

‹‹ Mark for once be honest with yourself and face reality. You don't want to have children for the simple reason that you are afraid that they might be born sick or that they might grow up as one of the undesirables that you fight with your dangerous criminal association!›› he shouted in my face, venting all the rage that had been suppressed until that moment. ‹‹ Don't mess with the association with the fact that I don't want to have children!››

‹‹ When we got engaged we always discussed enlarging the family and even after marriage or maybe the mister forgot?››

‹‹ Finished with the recriminations?›› and I escaped a giggle of derision. The straw that broke the camel's back. She snapped out of her chair and ran to barricade herself inside the bedroom, chiding me that the association had changed me. That reaction was due to my previous arrogance, but the pride of not giving in to those provocations was stronger than the understanding towards her, so: ‹‹ Lorelain what the fuck are you saying! Get out of that room and let me talk!››

I banged my fists against the door and kept yelling at her to get out and take back all those lies. I didn't want to have kids, that was the plain truth! I DON'T WANT TO HAVE KIDS! I DON'T WANT TO HAVE CHILDREN WHETHER YOU LIKE IT OR NOT...YOU WILL RESPECT MY WISHES!

Redemption days

Shitty night!

Lorelain stopped crying, but wouldn't open the door for me to come in. I had to fall back on the couch, which was uncomfortable, narrow, and short. I took some tablecloths from the pantry to cover myself on that cold and lonely night. Furthermore, I had not hidden anything from her, nor had I changed my mind. The remorse for those words, used in anger against her, continued to rumble in my head with every smallest and most painful pulsation. I shouldn't have lost my temper like that, nor should I have taken my anger and frustration out on her. We still loved each other very much... I still loved her as I did all those years ago... but what about her? No sound came from the other side of the room, she had fallen asleep, or maybe she was silent, alone with her thoughts. I imagined her, lying on the double bed, in the dark of the room with that little bit of light that managed to filter through the shutters creating that little optical effect at the base of the bed that sometimes frightened her.

He knew nothing about my life before we met. I hadn't been changed by my friends or even the association. From the period of my youth, I have memories clouded by the fumes of alcohol and reefer, not to mention the periods of frustration. When I was attending university, I shared a small apartment with three other guys, all students away from home like me, and we supported ourselves with small jobs (the same ones I found immediately after graduation). We studied (little), worked (little), and had fun (a lot), all based on sex, alcohol, and smoking. At our parties, all participants enjoyed themselves, not to mention all the girls who 'passed under us', which always returned to redo a second round on the rides. Every so often, some sentimental stories were born, which ended very quickly. Everything was going well, until the echoes of our goliardery reached the ears of my father: an old-fashioned man of advanced age, because he had had me at the threshold of sixty years, and in whose past were not contemplated alcohol, smoking, or premarital sex who wanted these rules to be respected by his son.

Redemption days

One morning I found him in front of the door of the apartment that almost came down with the blows he gave him. The night before there had been yet another party, and the apartment was in a sorry state, to say the least, to which we had become accustomed. Empty bottles scattered all over the house, food residue, dirty dishes and glasses, clothes left on the floor, and drunk people sleeping in every corner of the house. One even inside the bathtub! The mess woke Joseph up, and he headed to the front door to find out who the fucker was that was making all that noise so early in the morning (actually, dawn had passed about 10 hours ago). He opened the door and had the impression of being run over by a truck. He fell and hit his head against the wall, but luckily he was still anesthetized from the alcohol he had ingested during the party.

‹‹ Where are you hiding, you damned loafer!›› the intruder shouted, trying to frame me among the unconscious bodies of the guests.

‹‹ Damn, Dad, what the hell are you doing here?›› I said, leaving the room. His tone was unmistakable, and I would have been able to recognize him in any situation. The state in which I found myself did not work in my favor, perhaps it increased his anger toward me. I was wearing a T-shirt 'decorated' with some medal of I don't know what, white briefs and the shape of the pillow stuck to my face: ‹‹ You dirty bastard! You're a disgrace to the family... you ...›› he didn't even finish the sentence, and he lashed out at me, grabbing me by the shirt and dragging me into the bedroom, closing the door behind us. Those present at the scene did not move a finger to get me out of the way, considering their state of ethyl coma, what should I have expected? Unfortunately, in the room, I was not alone, but there was also a blonde, shapely and semi-naked who had succumbed to my courtship, making that night unforgettable. The fury didn't spare her, and she ran away, covering her nudity with the few clothes she managed to retrieve from the floor and was never seen again. Now we were facing each other. There had never been good blood between us, and that day the fragile bridge that still held us together was shattered.

‹‹ Do you think this is the way to enter other people's homes?››
‹‹ Don't you dare speak to me... you debauched of a son!››
‹‹ Debauched?››

Redemption days

‹‹ All those rumors concerning your unhealthy behavior... all true! You are a disgrace to the good name of the family! You've managed to dishonor us in front of the whole country!›› and he unleashed a right-hand worthy of a skilled boxer (even though he was old, he still had the energy to spare) that catapulted me backward, causing a severe cut on my upper lip. That punch had the merit of removing the numbness from my body, so I faced him for the first and last time in my life.

‹‹ Don't you dare put your hands on me! I live in this house, and what I do within these walls is my business and no one else's!››

‹‹ Don't you dare disrespect me! I'm your father, you little bastard!››

‹‹ What the fuck are you ranting about, you old man's prick! Respect? Do you talk about respect? You come storming into my house, almost kicking down the door, terrorizing my girlfriend, and punching me… and then you talk about respect? Fuck you, you filthy shit!›› and I saw him preparing to give me a second dose of respect accompanied by his "fatherly affection" but I caught him off guard. I dodged the punch and reacted by smacking him right in the face. He fell to the ground like a sack of potatoes with a somber thud. Even in that inferiority position, he didn't stop taunting me and hurling insults at me. Finally, I pulled him up by the lapels of his jacket, and with decisive action, I bent my arm behind his back and accompanied him to the door determined to throw him out of the house. Passing through the living room, I noticed that it had been emptied by the people who had bivouacked there the night before. I urged him not to be seen again, and he responded with a few sentences about my conduct, shouting at me that he was dead to him as a son and that I should forget about the money and the inheritance. That threat didn't scare me in the least, I would have continued to support myself with odd jobs, and I yelled at him that he could shove his money and his good thoughts up his ass and that I didn't need his lousy charity! I was going to finish my studies and get my degree in his face!

Redemption days

From that day on, my life took a different path from the one I had imagined as a child, but maybe it was the one destiny had reserved for me. The only contacts I had were with my mother, and all of them were in secret from my father, otherwise, he could have taken it out on that poor woman. I had the opportunity for redemption two years later, at my graduation, because even without financial help from her, I managed to complete my studies; no one showed up at the discussion of the thesis, but I received a letter from my mother with some marks inside (a small thought) and some words of encouragement for the future. The first days after graduation was quite hard, then came the turning point. I applied for a job in a well-known Berlin company and after passing the interview, I was hired in the main office, then came to the United States and my new life overseas. My mother didn't take the news very well, even though she knew in her heart that I was leaving to build a better future for myself, and I met her secretly before leaving her forever. A heartbreaking farewell that I will remember until the day I die.

My wife thought it was my new American friends who had led me astray, but she was wrong and perhaps suspected it, but she preferred to keep her blinkers on. Those ideas had been rooted in me since I was a teenager, I had them before and after marriage, unfortunately, I had not found a political outlet to manifest them openly, something that happened in the United States with the American Nation. She would never have admitted it, it was easier to think that it was my first American friendship that made me change and not that she had married a right-wing extremist. That nefarious night was drawing to a close. My bones ached and even my mood was at a low point. I hadn't stopped thinking about her... about finding a solution to regain the harmony lost in the marriage. The first rays of sunlight began to penetrate the room, illuminating the furniture little by little and at the same time breaking through the darkness that had surrounded me until that moment. From the other room, there were no noises, not even a hiss of breathing, nothing. Maybe he was finally sleeping deeply after the sleepless night spent thinking about the whole thing and asking himself the same questions as me, or at least that was what I wanted, but in reality, what had he thought or felt? After the anger, the thoughts, the memories, the reasoning made an appearance, the guilt. I was still reflecting on the situation when I heard the bedroom door open and I caught a glimpse of her in the half-light. I pretended to be asleep, resisted for a few seconds before bursting out: ‹‹ Please forgive me!››

I got up from the couch, dropping the tablecloths used as makeshift blankets, she stopped in front of me and I noticed she was wearing the same clothes as the night before. She had not changed.

‹‹ We have to decide,›› she replied.

Redemption days

Her tone was calm and flat. Devoid of emotion. My legs gave out, and I fell back to sitting on the couch. We had to decide on our future, but she had already made up her mind. She spoke of her nightly reflections, of the thousands of questions she had asked herself after our quarrel between tears of anger and pain and despair. I listened in silence. I didn't dare look up at her. Furthermore, I kept staring at one spot in the room. I didn't dare to face her inquisitive eyes filled with pity for the wretch she had married. I went to work anyway, even though my state of mind was not the best, but I did it to keep my mind off her speech. I worked mechanically, in a listless way, I tried to listen to other people's speeches but from their mouths only laconic 'blah, blah' came out, repetitive and meaningless. I nodded, denied, affirmed this or that, but nothing more. In the evening I returned home with a sense of melancholy, but as a sign of reconciliation, I bought a dozen red roses, the most expensive in the store.

I found the house empty. She was gone. She had left me only a note with a few words written on it, advising me of her return to her parent's house for a period of reflection. I threw the bouquet of roses in the trash, along with that damned note. I did nothing, not even a call to find out how she was or to convince her to retrace her steps. The thin thread that bound us together was by now worn out and torn in several places, and it would have taken only the slightest tug to make it break for good, a situation that I wanted to avoid with every means in my possession. My whole life was falling into a dark and cold abyss, and I still didn't see the light of salvation. I used an old method (ultra-tested) to try to forget my problems, at least for a few hours, that is I stuck to the bottle and I did it also the following evenings, in the living room, lying on the couch and with the cell phone at my side in the vain expectation of a call from him. With every sip of liquor, my gaze fell hopelessly on the picture of the two of us from that famous weekend, where everything originated. If I had had the chance to go back to the past, I would have certainly behaved differently, unfortunately, I did not have that power yet, and down I went to drain my second bottle of liquor. In those lonely twilight in the company of the bottles, I had the temptation to dial the phone number to talk to her and ask her forgiveness, but the alcohol prevented me from doing so. I couldn't give in first, she had to be the one to put aside her ridiculous suffragette-style feminist pride and come back to me with her tail between her legs. It would be at that very moment that I would dictate my terms of peace, and they would all be in my favor. I just had to stand my ground.

Redemption days

It wasn't easy. I avoided everyone, ignoring everything that was going on in the outside world, and the few people who tried to make any contact, I pushed them away in a bad way, until I managed to make scorched earth around me. Nobody knew the reason for my state of mind, and nobody would find out. Another drink...more thoughts...the phone remained silent.

One morning, James came to my office to ask for advice about a file he had been following for several days that had, unfortunately, got stuck. I didn't welcome him in the best way, he had put it on the bill, by now all the office was talking about nothing else but my change of character.

‹‹ Sorry to disturb you.››

‹‹ What do you want?››

‹‹ If you're busy, I can come back in a few minutes.››

‹‹ Later on, it will be the same, so tell me what you have to say and then try to disappear, understand?››

‹‹ I wanted to ask you about a practice that has stalled,›› I stared into his eyes for a long time, then I said: "You make a mess, and then you come to me whining like a bitch to get your chestnuts out of the fire, right?

‹‹ No... you see...›› she tried to answer the accusation, but I could see she didn't know what to say. He felt uncomfortable.

‹‹ Do me a favor. Leave me a note and if I have the time and the inclination I'll check it, if not, do it yourself and now get lost!››

James did not reply. He left my office, apologizing for the disturbance, only after he had gone away, did I read the yellow post-it note he had left me. What I read surprised me greatly. "If you want to confide?" I had treated him like shit and with such superiority that anyone would have told me to fuck off, without a second thought. He had extended his hand to help me, I needed no help and no desire to confide in anyone, least of all him. Since I had run out of alcohol in the house, before going home, I used to stop by some bar to drink something strong.

In the meantime, Lorelain had not yet decided to make herself heard: not even a message on the answering machine, nor a text message. I resisted but once I almost gave in to the desire to hear from her to put an end to the whole thing I began to dial her cell phone number, but then I thought better of it and closed the phone. Our house (once, our love nest), well-kept and clean, was acquiring a scruffy and lonely aspect that reflected my state of mind. I sat on the couch with the TV on, tuned to whatever channel was on, silent. In my hand was the tenth beer to drink, which would have reached the previous cans on the floor. Scattered on the floor, empty, some intact and some misshapen. The only light on in the entire house was the one in the bedroom. Brightly lit.

Suddenly the silence was interrupted by the ringing of the phone, once a familiar sound and now almost completely unknown. I waited until the fifth ring then I answered, hoping it was the long-awaited call, but instead: ‹‹ Hello, how are you?›› it wasn't her.

‹‹ Hello... we continue to live and you?››

Redemption days

‹‹ Well, but given the tone... are you sure you're okay?›› (tone from beyond the grave) ‹‹ The start of flu. Any news from the association or a courtesy call?››

‹‹ Both.››

‹‹ Come on, Matt, cut to the chase!›› He briefed me on the latest events of the war for power we were fighting, but honestly, after the latest personal events, the temptation to blow it all was growing inside of me, but the thirst for power was getting the better of me. Matt and John along with six other members wanted to organize a counter move to try to convert other members to our cause, so what was better than organizing a demonstration act against 'half men'? Nothing! It was a good choice since the action performed by Rat-Face against that club of transvestites had attracted many undecided about his political current. The action would take place the following night, the target had been identified and properly controlled. Let's say that the plan was the same as the competition's, throwing Molotov cocktails inside the club to set it on fire and cause as many victims as possible. A bit of fun would certainly have lifted my spirits and I would have forgotten my marital woes for a while.

On the night of the demonstration, we found ourselves at the chosen location, two blocks from the venue. In total there were six participants in the raid (including myself) and we had three cars at our disposal. About ten incendiary bottles were ready to be lit and thrown inside that damned perverted place for a healthy purification with flames. That night I discovered that it wasn't a real nightclub but an association in support of those beings but for us, it didn't change anything whether it was a nightclub or a support association or a brothel, the purpose was the same: to kill them all and punish them for their disease. That association was located in a two-story apartment building. The ground floor and the second floor were occupied by the offices and meeting places of the association, while on the second floor no one lived it had been vacant for some time, who would go to live above that shitty hangout? Nobody in their right mind! The entrance was located on the main street, with houses and stores (all closed at that time), a narrow one-way street. Two nice large windows would have favored the entrance of our warm greetings. A secondary entrance was in the first side street on the left, at the first intersection coming from Cobet Main Street.

Redemption days

A dark (little street lighting) and closed alley, and no windows. Even from that point, we would have been able to throw a few bottles inside, so on the block the only way out to those pigs. A car was placed not even one meter away from the main entrance, positioned in such a way to be able to better observe the movements of the people without being too conspicuous and ready to go into action. Another one was parked far from the place, to act as a lookout and the last one was in the secondary alley. The drivers chosen were good, in emergencies they were very good at escaping and losing the police cars; I was in the car in the alley, John was in the one in the main street and Matt was in the 'lookout' car. The contacts between the three teams were secured with cell phones bought from fences for a few dollars and cards... new and purchased by providing fake data, since once the goal was achieved everything would be burned to erase the evidence. Normal conversations for outsiders (in case of eavesdropping) but not for us. Well-charged cell phones, with earphones on to keep your hands free from entanglements, and at that point, you could start Operation 'Purifying Fire'.

‹‹ John, how's the weather looking? Where I come from, it's calm.››

‹‹ It's quiet, but I see rain clouds approaching ›› unfortunately for us, a group of people was approaching the entrance, so we had to wait for them to disappear. In the alley all was quiet, not a soul was around... too bad! I wanted to act when suddenly the iron door opened, illuminating a part of the alley with the light coming from inside. Change of plan! Two figures came out. We stayed in the car, hidden in the darkness. The only solution was to observe the development of the situation. I immediately warned John and Matt of the technical problems that were disturbing our transmissions, and they both understood the situation and decided to wait a little longer: if the situation did not change, the operation would be blown. The two of them were still in front of the entrance, I could see very little from that position, but I noticed that they were hugging each other as if it was a normal thing, and then they kissed! At that point I wanted to get out of the car, run towards them wielding a metal rod and hit them repeatedly until I saw them fall into a lake of blood... of their blood and then stick it into their filthy broken ass... so they could try something hard! We were in danger of being caught, and both John and Matt insisted on abandoning the operation, but decided on a few more minutes of waiting. One of the two sickos froze right in our direction.

Eternal seconds.

Redemption days

Had that bastard eaten the leaf? Inside the cockpit, we remained silent, almost not breathing for fear of being heard. The driver put his fingers on the keys, ready to go full throttle to escape. The tension was slicing through him. I stopped him. Alarm reset. He kissed the other one on the mouth and said a few sentences, and then drove off in our direction. Damn it! I ordered us to stay still and in the dark, he would have passed by us, but I was sure he wouldn't have noticed our presence. I followed the bastard with my eyes, until the exit of the alley, perhaps to reassure me of his disappearance while the other did not want to hear about it to go back inside. At that point, it would have been his cocks! He would have acted the same. In the end, but, he went back in, closing the door behind him. The countdown could begin.

‹‹ Ten... Nine... Eight...››

John and his group would leave first, then it would be my team's turn.

‹‹ Seven... Six...›› everything was going well.

‹‹ Five... Four...››

Perhaps the attack wouldn't bear the desired fruit, but we would be able to bring more affiliates to our side.

‹‹ Three... Two... and...››

Let's start playing... ‹‹ Stop! Stop everything! Abortion! Fuck!››

Two headlights illuminated from behind the alley, and in front of that car ran a figure. A man. Strange and unusual situation.

‹‹ Matt, quickly leave your post! Warn the others.››

‹‹ What's going on? Everything all right?››

‹‹ Leave!››

‹‹ Roger!››

Redemption days

That intrusion had dealt the final blow to the bombing, but I didn't give the order to fall back for my team yet, I wanted to observe that strange scene. The car had a moderate pace, it didn't want to kill the running man, it almost looked like it wanted to push him right into the alley to trap him. They both passed us, without us noticing, their attention was focused on the chase. The figure continued to run toward the alley and when he reached about the height of the metal door, he slammed into it. The car accelerated until it came to a halt right in front of the two steps that separated it from the figure. A frightening figure, who did not know what would happen to her that night. The man had the strength to scream, the terror had blocked him and... a fury came out of the car and hurled itself against him, grabbed him by the neck and after having lifted him from the ground, threw him over the hood (which still had the engine running) producing a dry and metallic thud, then the victim fell to the ground. He was trying to get up to flee but the encounter with the hood first and with the hard ground later, had stunned him, he could not coordinate his movements. The tormentor did not waste time and attacked him with kicks and punches, insulting him heavily. The poor guy tried in vain to protect himself from that fury until he had no more reaction. I don't know what came over me at that moment, I should have given the order to leave that alley, but I did the opposite... I ordered my driver to stay, I got out of the car and headed towards the two individuals fighting. Furthermore, I grabbed the attacker from behind and tried to block him or at least get him away from the victim, and I realized that it was quite a difficult task. I finally achieved my goal and blocked him completely.

I still couldn't frame the two main actors, but I noticed that the car he got out of, after a quick reverse and a U-turn, left the alley and entered the main street, but what I never expected was the abandonment of my brother at the wheel: That dirty bastard had followed the other car's example and dumped me (for no reason) in that alley, in the company of a crazy murderer and at the risk of finding myself surrounded by fags and feds. He would have paid dearly, and yes... he would have paid dearly, that son of a bitch!

‹‹ It's a personal matter! Stay the fuck out of it!›› I let go. That voice was none other than...

‹‹ John? What the fuck is wrong with you? You bastard, you're nothing else!›› I told him while I was pulling him, turning him towards me. For his part, he answered with force to my intrusion: ‹‹ I tell you again! Private matter! So get the fuck out!››

‹‹ Damn you! Do you realize that you have ruined the operation? And it's none of my business? For fuck's sake, calm down before someone comes or worse the cops!›› and I pushed him away even more from the other one, who was still on the ground, trembling and dirty with blood clotting various parts of his face. His shirt was torn in some places, and the knuckles of his hands peeled due to the blows received in an attempt to defend himself.

‹‹ Stop... please dad... stop!››

That trembling, frightening figure was his son! Arthur! After that night, John was untraceable for a good two weeks. He didn't answer his phone or his cell phone. Two weeks of oblivion for him and his family!

Redemption days

One evening I found him in front of the house waiting for me for more than an hour. I was returning from my usual round of drinks when I recognized him. As soon as he saw me, he approached me hesitantly, and I noticed that now and then he would glance in all directions as if he was afraid of being followed. I made him sit in the house, but his stealthy attitude did not change, he was standing in the middle of the living room nervously gesticulating with his hands.

‹‹ Sit down and relax... you're as tense as a violin string,›› I said as I went to the kitchen to get two bottles of beer from the fridge. I guessed the reason for the visit and I didn't want to know anything or be put in the middle of it, it was personal and private business. But I couldn't send him away either, he needed help, and I wasn't going to back down.
‹‹ Tell me everything, come on" and I handed him the bottle of beer that he took mechanically laying it immediately on the table, without even opening it.

‹‹ It's about that cursed night...›› he began trembling.

He could not look me in the eyes. The shame of what had happened prevented him from facing my gaze. I said again that he didn't have to talk about it if he didn't feel like it, it was an internal matter of his family, but he didn't accept the invitation, he had to confide in someone otherwise he could have exploded!

‹‹ It was a trap! That bastard orchestrated the whole thing!››
‹‹ Rat-face.››

So my direct competitor was resorting to low blows to take me out of the presidential race, moreover hitting my closest friends? Son of a bitch! The director was not him but Oscar Bell, a spineless, small, stocky homunculus who had not even joined the American Nation for a year and was already embroiled in the war for power. I wondered what "Rat-Face" could have promised him to get him on his side and set up that infamous trap against John. Maybe a career advancement within the association, which would be realized only when he became president, or something else? John said that the idea came from Oscar, who at first should not have participated actively in the action, but when one of the three drivers stood up, Oscar stepped in to replace him.

John didn't think that behavior was strange, so he didn't suspect anything, and thinking back I would have done the same. The idea was great, so why not make it happen? Unfortunately for him and us, the henchmen of "Rat Face" in the days before the initiative, had followed Arthur looking for a weak point to use as a weapon against us, and they found it! A family tragedy that also directly involved the entire association and its precarious internal political balance. John continued in his story: ‹‹ Three days after that night, I received a peremptory order to present myself to the chief for a meeting of two for a delicate and urgent matter. Such a summons could only mean an infamous expulsion from the association,›› I nodded. Unfortunately, he was right.

‹‹ I'll spare you all the discussion I had with the boss, or rather, his monologue since he wouldn't let me speak. In conclusion, my expulsion will be examined!››

Redemption days

A predictable ending, but at that point, the political battle had turned into a personal matter.

‹‹ We'll do everything to prevent it, trust me, we won't leave you alone.››
‹‹ Thank you, unfortunately, my fate is sealed. You know very well that they will take advantage of Arthur and... his... illness!››

Up to that moment he had held back from saying this, but now he was beginning to realize the serious state of his son's health. Then to find out about the disease in that way...fuck...would have destroyed anyone. He confessed that he hadn't erased the events of that night from his mind, he couldn't...he could see Arthur kissing and grinding like a whore in heat with that other pervert in that filthy alley. In the street...in front of the world, shamelessly, how disgusting! How repugnant! The son must have been worse off than his father, the beatings he had taken that night were just the appetizer for a bunch of punches and kicks.

After the cars had fled, it was just the three of us left in the alley. On foot and without our cell phones because in the confusion we had forgotten them in our cars. John's anger towards his unworthy son faded, also because we would have run the risk of finding ourselves talking in front of his tombstone... which would not have been a bad thing. No one had run out to see what the commotion was about. We found out later that during the chase and the beating, there were only four members inside the association, going about their business, and it was the norm there to hear cars crashing at night, and no one called the authorities. In the meantime, Matt, who in the meantime had understood the real situation, decided to intervene and substituted his companion at the wheel, while he left with another car. He was the one who lifted that little, reckless man off the ground, while I tried to calm his father down further. Arthur didn't say a word or make a sound the whole way to the car, just touching the painful parts of his face. Matt put his arm around his waist and helped him sit in the back. I drove and John sat by my side, while Matt was in the back seat with the degenerate. First, we stopped at John's house, then mine, and before we got off, Matt and I promised not to tell anyone about that night.

‹‹ The family situation?›› I asked to get information and understand how the case had evolved once we got home.

‹‹ How do you want it to go?›› he answered disconsolately, then resumed: ‹‹The problem is in the association. You're losing to that scoundrel... it makes me so angry... what a fool I was, I should have realized what was happening around me right away... instead... excuse me...›› he got up from the sofa and started walking.

Redemption days

‹‹ Come on, don't blame yourself, and we can still make up for it, but you have to focus on your home, that's where the real drama is. How did Mary take the news of her illness?›› and I begged him to sit down, his pacing made me nervous. ‹‹ Mary... poor woman. As soon as he saw us cross the threshold in that condition, he asked for an explanation and tried to hold him to see if he needed help, but that being... nothing. He gave her a push to move away and almost knocked her down. I swear to you... I would have punched him again... Furthermore, I held back only for Mary. The guy was already holed up in his room, so I took the opportunity to tell her everything, and... she cried. She couldn't help herself. The poor woman didn't know what to do to save him from the eternal flames.››

Poor family!

‹‹ At first she couldn't believe that Arthur was sick and depraved and that maybe I was wrong, you know in the dark and other such excuses, but in the end, she didn't believe what was coming out of his mouth either. Inside, she had known very well for a long time the curse that was growing in Arthur, but she refused to admit it openly. A kind of self-defense. She has always been a woman of sound principles and capable of reasoning even in situations of emergency and strong emotional stress... you know that too, so after initial bewilderment, she had already prepared a way out.›› Mary's decision consisted in forcibly hospitalizing the patient in a specialist clinic, where he would be treated with all the necessary care, until his complete recovery. Even before meeting John, she was already dedicated to raising awareness against this disease, even if the world organization of doctors did not recognize it as such (thanks to their lobbies of power!), through a Catholic association that dealt with these recoveries and the healing of the sick, which was based on the studies and method of healing of a well-known luminary of science, Dr. Nicolosi. The association would handle the transfer to the center, anonymously and confidentially, to avoid hype, so they decided to act that very night. Mary called a member of her association and explained to him the drama her family had been plunged into. Within two hours, Arthur was brought to safety, ready to begin the healing process. The parents entered their son's room immediately after his transfer to pack a suitcase with some clothes and at that moment they realized that their lives had changed. The room bore some signs of struggle, the books in the small bookcase were all on the floor, the desk chair overturned and the bed unmade as if he had been clinging to it to prevent being taken away. They found the cell phone in the corner of the room and turned it on. John took it in his hands and started scrolling through

Redemption days

the address book, where most of the names were male... what a rage! Then he read some text messages, and at that point, he threw the phone against the wall with such impetus that he smashed it completely. She didn't care about her husband's gesture and continued packing her suitcase. She chose her clothes with care as if her son were going on a vacation to some exotic destination. Even though he was not her natural son, she loved him with all her heart and wanted to see him heal. Suddenly she had to sit on the edge of the bed to catch her breath. All the commotion had fatigued her and given her pregnant state, that was not a good sign. John asked her if she was okay, she nodded her head in the affirmative, but her eyes betrayed her. She was crying. John sat down next to her and held her in a warm embrace. The next morning they brought the clothes to their son and John wanted to see him in person, at first they denied him the meeting then they agreed to let him meet her, and so they found themselves face to face. One in front of the other, inside a sterile, white room of the medical center. In silence. Arthur stared into his eyes, he didn't say anything while his father tried to reassure him stating that they were doing it for his good, then... something snapped in the boy that turned into a bloodthirsty beast.

He lashed out at his father, shouting insults at him. Fortunately, the nurses present stopped him just in time and gave him a massive dose of tranquilizer. John was shocked by that vision, he would have never, ever expected such a reaction from his son, it was clear that he was sick and in pain. The hospitalization and those treatments would have helped him to heal, he was doing it for his good and one day Arthur would have understood it too, yes... he would have understood it if he had found a woman who would have made him happy and a father... now he did not realize it. He left the room, not looking back. The doctor forbade visits for two weeks, given Arthur's reaction to him, which could thwart his progress toward recovery. John stayed in the doctor's private office for about an hour and learned useful information from the doctor about his son's state of health. Arthur was not homosexual, but a latent heterosexual. The doctor asked John about some details of his family life and so he told about his divorce, his absence from home because of gambling, his divorce from his first wife, and his recent rapprochement with his son; in the end, the doctor came to the conclusion that his absence from his son's life had made him weak in the face of the countless attacks from the so-called homosexual lobbies, whose main purpose was to make homosexuality appear normal, and that perhaps during his absence Arthur had looked elsewhere for a fatherly and masculine figure, turning to the wrong person. Arthur had been led astray by one of them and pushed to believe he was homosexual, this was the doctor's verdict. John did not rest and blamed himself for his son's illness, poor man. A sad and tragic story. He told me that according to him, his son had been seeing someone for some time, and unfortunately, he had not yet been able to understand who it was.

Redemption days

That evening he had come to me to ask for help in finding the bastard who had led the boy astray to punish him and render him harmless. He was never to harm anyone else again. I asked what his ex-wife thought of the whole affair, and he calmly told me that he had settled everything by inventing a plausible excuse and that she had believed him. Before leaving, I promised him that I would be at his side in the search for that bastard and that once I had him in my hands, he would bitterly regret what he had done to Arthur. When I was left alone, doubt and fear assailed me.

The next day I spent thinking about the story of John and his son, and honestly, I did not know where to start. I worked as always, but that evening I avoided going to the usual bar, coming home early to eat, unfortunately, but when I opened the fridge I was surprised to find it empty. Without realizing it I had finished all the food, forgetting to do the shopping, because when Lorelain was there, she took care of it. I didn't lose heart and decided to go to Ed's diner. I arrived just in time for dinner. Outside the diner was a sign with the menu of the day and some house specials with the cheapest prices in the entire state, at least that's what the handwriting at the base of the sign said. At the cash register, located at the entrance, I found (as always) Ed's wife. A mountain of flaccid fat, sitting on a tiny stool from which her huge ass was sticking out. Not even a quarter of a single butt could fit on top of the stool. At least she could get that damn hairnet off her head when she was at the checkout counter, and a shower wouldn't hurt her at all, considering the grease and sweat dripping down both sides of her arms. I greeted her and asked if there were free tables for dinner, she nodded her head in affirmative and said: ‹‹ I think so, today we have had our fill of customers, but if you wait a moment, I'll find out.›› She lifted the receiver of an old telephone and dialed an internal number.

‹‹ Today is your lucky day, a table has just opened up, take a seat in the dining room, and a waitress will go with you. Enjoy your meal.›› and I entered the room… semi-deserted. I was not even entering the most "IN" and expensive place in town.

Redemption days

A brunette girl with, an angelic face with a light make-up on her face and a uniform that left nothing to the imagination (a fourth of sill!) stood in front of me and kindly let me sit at the table, leaving me the menu of the place, worn and greasy, within evidence the house dish: 'Grilled steak with potatoes' at the modest price of 3.58 dollars, or you could opt, always for that amount, for a first course and a salad. The restaurant was not very clean or aesthetically pleasing, but Ed's cooking was excellent, and the prices rarely exceeded 10 dollars. The patrons of this place were single, divorced, single men without a woman, and all of a certain age. The only conversations that could be overheard were those of the customers with the waitresses for the orders. As soon as I decided what to eat, I motioned to the waitress, who immediately approached, showing off her order pad and that lovely rack of hers.

‹‹ I would like the house specialty, the one for $3.58, and to drink a bottle of beer, ice-cold, please››.

I handed her the menu; she took it but pointed out that there were two specials at that price, so?
‹‹ Excuse me, you are right. I will have the meat with potatoes, please››.
‹‹ It goes well, but it wants to order the other?››
‹‹ No, thank you. That's fine.›› Fast service and great food.

You could see from a mile away that it had been several days since I had tasted a decent dish because I had rushed like a hyena on the carcass of a dead animal. I paid at the cashier's desk, but I made sure to leave the girl a large tip, I distrusted the big woman, then I went home and as soon as I crossed the threshold I noticed a red "1" flashing on the answering machine. Only one message. I put the keys to the side and pressed the button. Click!

Redemption days

The message started: 'Hi, it's me. Mark this number. 555-752015. It's my lawyer's, call him!' I replayed that damn message I don't know how many times. I felt like shit! Furthermore, I didn't know what to do... think... the world was crashing down on top of my head and I couldn't stop it! Why was he doing this? Not even the courage to face me in person and tell me he wanted a divorce! I knew very well that behind that decision there was the hand of the mother, who had never put up with me, and for sure that wicked woman was toasting to her daughter's freedom from that cruel ogre of a husband. I exploded with rage! I ran into the bedroom and opened her closet for the first time since she left me (she had insisted on buying two separate closets) and found it empty. Other than the bare essentials, she had taken everything out without my knowledge. I thought it was a passing crisis, a quick return, but it was the opposite. Since that damn morning, she had made her final decision! The anger exploded and focused on the empty closet. I began to kick and punch the doors closed. My hands began to hurt, but I didn't stop. The damage was insignificant, so I grabbed a chair and used it as a weapon to destroy it, but it was still not enough, so I retrieved a large hammer from the toolbox and dedicated myself to the demolition of the hated desire of my now ex-wife. Little by little, blow-by-blow, it began to give way. Pieces flew from all over the room and sweat made its appearance on my temples and my face distorted with every blow inflicted. A few more blows and it would have collapsed for good: at that point, I would have laughed out loud, in the face of that bitch! I snickered as I saw the result of my revenge, but then the laughter became tears of despair at the abandonment of my wife.

About ten days went by, all similar to each other, and I hadn't called that number, and wouldn't.

Unfortunately, the search for the bastard had not yielded any results. We managed to get into Arthur's email (thanks to a hacker friend of ours) and Facebook profile, but we couldn't find any useful sign of recognition. John occasionally kept me updated on his son's health. From what the doctors were telling him, the boy had started to cooperate, and the treatment was giving the first signs of recovery to the joy of his parents, thus re-balancing the balance of life. One morning, as I was briskly crossing the hallway to the bathroom, I passed James and quickly greeted him. It was only later that I realized that the boy did not look well and that it was the first time I had seen him since my last rant at him in my office. I entered the first free bathroom and was finally able to empty my bladder just in time. If I had stopped to talk to James, sure I would have peed my pants!

‹‹ Hello!››

‹‹ Holy shit. James››.

I found him standing in front of the toilet door waiting for me to come out, and I don't think he wanted to use it for his needs.

‹‹ James...do you want me dead? You scared me, come on... what are you waiting for?››

‹‹ You. I'd like to talk to you.››

‹‹ If you want to talk to me about that practice... go ahead››

‹‹ No work. Issue resolved, thank you.››

Redemption days

‹‹ So?›› I asked as I washed my hands in the sink.

‹‹ It's a private matter››.

‹‹ We can go to my office, so we will be quiet.››

‹‹ I'd prefer to go out of the office if it's not a problem for you››.

‹‹ No problem I have to forgive the treatment not being elegant last time, so we can do it this evening after work, at the usual place, okay?››

‹‹ OK. Tonight at the usual place. Thanks›› and left me in front of the bathroom mirror.

That evening I would have put my problems in the attic and I would have regretted him to raise him a little moral. The work had accumulated on the desk, batteries, and piles of files, arranged as good and better that they had to be processed as soon as possible; The difficulty was not in the number but the little desire I found myself. I couldn't do anything but take the first of the series and start giving us inside. For the fault of those damned practices, I reached ten minutes late to the appointment with James and as always the place was full of people, but I managed the same to see it and to reach it at the table. Fortunately, the boy had already ordered a strange blue drink.

‹‹ Hi James, sorry I'm late, but the paperwork has piled up. I see you've already had your drink, good man››.

‹‹ I'm sorry... I would have ordered for you, but I didn't know what you preferred.››

‹‹ No problem, I would have done the same in your place. Busy night, isn't it?››

‹‹ What kind of drink did you have?››

‹‹ A lousy one with an unpronounceable name. Trust the bartender››

‹‹ A piece of advice... next time order a nice mug of beer and be sure to fall on your feet››.

‹‹ Next time...››

The waiter brought us two impressive mugs of beer, one blonde for James and the other black for yours truly, which I had ordered at the counter before sitting down at the table.

‹‹ Thanks for the beer, so I can rinse my mouth from that disgusting drink. Occasionally you have to try something new...››

‹‹ Now and then, right? But first, you have to find out about the ingredients. So how are you? You look very worried. Work matters?›› I said, sipping my beer while the boy put aside his drink to throw himself on his mug.

‹‹ Work is going well, then I'm quite settled in the office. Thanks for your interest››.

It was a difficult conversation to start, he couldn't manage to unblock himself, even though it was clear that he wanted to get something off his chest. Unfortunately, her distrust of me was still high, so I made the first move that cost me a lot from an emotional point of view.

‹‹ My wife asked me for a divorce,›› I said in a tone as natural as possible. He was struck by that statement.

‹‹ I'm sorry. I don't know what to say... maybe it wasn't the right time to go out, given your situation.››

Redemption days

‹‹ It's okay, no problem. Even though it was a bolt out of the blue, I can say that I handled the blow quite well›› and I couldn't say the same for my ex's closet! I began to recount my marital misadventure, leaving out a few details that I considered unnecessary and uninteresting, and for the first time, I realized that I had taken the blame for the end of the marriage.

James listened to the whole affair in silence and only at the end expressed his opinion. Simple and direct: ‹‹ Talk to her and admit your mistakes by taking the first step. Each of us makes mistakes, whether they are big or small, it matters little but if you dare to face them head-on, you will always find a solution. You are still in time to recover the relationship with your wife››.

Sometimes confiding in a friendly person is very good for the soul and mood.

I got up from the table and hugged him, while he was still sitting in his seat. I had taken him by surprise with that gesture, and I was surprised as well. It was not my characteristic to embrace another man with such naturalness and feeling of gratitude, that was the prerogative of gays and not straights. The ringing of the cell phone brought me back to reality and I apologized to James for that gesture, and he understood. An unexpected call, given the time, must have been urgent and important. I apologized to James for the second time in the space of a few seconds and walked away from the table in search of a quieter place, where the reception notches were more than the two that were on the display. Finally, I went into the restroom and answered the 'anonymous' call no number had appeared. On the other end, I had the big boss on the line.

‹‹ Hello, boss. Any news?››

‹‹ Delicate, significant, and urgent news. I need to talk to you in person, show up tomorrow in my office at lunchtime. Be on time, please››, and closed the communication, without even giving me time to respond. Orders were not discussed. Once back at the table, I had the bitter surprise of being left alone. James was not to be found, he certainly had not gone to the bathroom, otherwise, I would have run into him, perhaps he had gone to the counter to order another drink... so I decided to sit and wait for him. Suddenly a waitress approached me and served me a beer and a note from James in which he apologized, but he had to run away, and not to worry about the bill because he had paid it and that we will update later. Patience, I was sorry for the conclusion of the evening, but in the end, I also drank that mug of beer for the health of the boy.

The meeting with the boss that was scheduled for lunchtime, had completely closed my stomach and at the same time put a certain uneasiness: surely the issue was important, and certainly, the break would not be enough, so to cover my ass I took two hours of leave. The office at that time was empty, perhaps only the boss and I were there, and I wasn't surprised by the choice of that time for the meeting. The boss wanted to make sure he didn't have any other people in the way. I knocked on the door.

‹‹ Come in!›› I heard from the other side. Furthermore, I walked into the study and greeted him warmly. He stared down at me, sitting in his pure leather executive chair with his ever-present Cuban cigar between his fingers.

Redemption days

‹‹ Welcome, darling, and I'm delighted you're on time. Good start,›› he said, consulting his wristwatch. A Rolex costing more than 10 thousand dollars, and yes, the old man was certainly not doing badly, quite the opposite.

‹‹ Have a seat, and we'll begin the discussion.››

‹‹ Thank you, boss.››

‹‹ John's situation is very critical, it grieves me, but I could not avoid taking measures against him, and there is another problem, which concerns you closely.

What do you mean? John's situation also concerns me closely... he is a very dear friend of mine and I will do everything I can to help him...››

‹‹ Let us give time to time. Your matter concerns the race for my succession and the internecine war that has been going on between you and... 'Rat-Face'!›› I was stunned. He knew my opponent's nickname, and who knows what else he knew.

‹‹ Don't be more surprised than you have to be, you also know that the bosses must be aware of every smallest and most insignificant detail to keep the internal balance calm and safe. As you must know, I am also aware of your impending divorce and the fact that your wife has been living in her parents' home for several weeks. Let's face it, in my opinion, you would make a great boss and a worthy successor of mine››

I didn't know whether to be happy about the compliments or pissed off about the leak.

‹‹ A leader can openly expose himself to a candidate, who must be careful to surround himself with people who are reliable and not blackmail-able from any point of view, and unfortunately this is not the case. As you may have understood, the problem is not about your divorce, because you would be in very good company, but about John. His case could prevent you from winning, just because of your friendship.›› He had a point, after all that doubt had flashed through my mind, but I had discarded it immediately.

‹‹ I can't blame poor John. I'd rather leave the chair to Rat-Face than leave my friend to his fate››.

The boss smiled at that statement, a sly smile of one who knew better. He got up from the armchair and went to the bar (always stocked with first-rate liquors) and prepared two whiskeys with ice. I took it and drank it in one gulp. He was on my side for the race for the presidency, but with reservations. He could not or did not want to expose himself more than necessary, perhaps because of the issue of John.

‹‹ Chief, let's be clear: John and his wife, after discovering their son's illness, did not lose heart and had him hospitalized for the necessary treatment, and I am sure he will make a full recovery, furthermore let's keep in mind that this whole story has come out of a boorish and cowardly plot orchestrated by 'Rat Face' to hit me. It will all deflate with time, I don't think it's the case to proceed against him. It takes time, and rest assured I'll shut up that homunculus Michael, too!››

Redemption days

Arguing in John's defense and more. I was gambling everything to continue the race, without further damaging my friend.

What you said makes no sense. Unfortunately, you lack the time!

‹‹ One month, I only need one month, I know it is risky but listen to me and give me your blessing for the good of the entire association. I can't think that you want to give the scepter to that madman who would surely sink the American Nation in one stroke!››

‹‹ The only move I can make is to postpone John's trial and that's it, I'm sorry.››

‹‹ Chief put your hand on your heart. John has been and is an active member of the association, he has never withdrawn from anything. You must help him concretely, listen to me. Do it for our common good!'››

The last appeal to save the association and dear John.

‹‹ Words spoken from the heart. Unfortunately, you have lost several points on your brothers and only John could help you recover them and lead you to victory.››

‹‹ John? But if he's risking being expelled, how could he help me win?››

‹‹ Didn't you start looking for that bastard who diverted his son?››

‹‹ Yes... but how does he know?››

‹‹ It doesn't matter, the important thing is that you find that being and that John is the one who will give him a good lesson after which you will have a clear path to the presidency and avoid expulsion from your friend. This is the only solution to your problem››.

I arrived about ten minutes early. The devil's advocate's office was very upscale, and the furniture always reminded you of that. Modern, linear, and expensive. It was easy to see that behind the layout and choice of furniture was the touch of a specialist interior designer. I sat in a small chair in the waiting room, ready for the call inside the arena, where I would be mauled by beasts. Uninteresting (from my point of view) magazines scattered elegantly over the glass coffee table and the secretary sitting at her checkpoint gave me disapproving sometimes looks as if she had already judged me and condemned me for the wreck of the marriage. The lawyer hadn't shown up yet, but I was alerted to his delay caused by a minor setback. I would have to wait another five minutes to see the end of that nightmare. At that moment she appeared. I found her in great shape, slightly aged but still disarmingly beautiful. As soon as she saw her, the secretary went to meet her and after the greetings made her sit inside the office, leaving me alone in the waiting room. We greeted each other with a single gesture of the head and nothing more. Seeing her after all that time brought back many memories, and I was so absorbed that I didn't even notice the appearance of the lawyer.

Redemption days

‹‹ Good evening. If you want to sit inside, we can start the meeting›› he made seriously and with the smell under his nose, indicating me to follow him. I apologized for the momentary distraction and entered the room, where Lorelain had already occupied one of the two available chairs. After much procrastination, I was now facing a nightmare for which I was not prepared. The lawyer asked me to sit down, and then immediately began to explain the situation. He outlined all the facts that had led to the divorce petition and then moved on to his side's demands. We remained silent and listened to him, now and then she nodded, while I cast a few timid glances in her direction in the vain hope of meeting her eyes to see if she still had any feelings towards me.

Useless.

She just stared at the lawyer.

‹‹ These are my client's requests... but I'm sorry... your lawyer? The invitation was extended to him if I'm not mistaken, wasn't it?›› he asked surprised as if he had noticed only at that very moment the lack of the other party. As an actor, he sucked!
‹‹ No lawyer. I'm not even thinking of getting one, I don't think there will be any problems in agreeing on the various legal and economic issues. I have no desire to start a war to the death, that's all››.

Direct and concise.

‹‹ So, if this is your decision, we take note of it. At this point I'll deliver you the documentation with my client's requests, so you can have a look and check them at your leisure›› and he handed me an envelope.

‹‹ Thank you››

‹‹ Then we could also arrange the next meeting if both parties agree.››

‹‹ No problem,›› I said.

‹‹ Go ahead and schedule it, thank you,›› Lorelain said.

‹‹ I was thinking of after Thanksgiving, the exact date... let's see... unfortunately I don't have my appointment book handy, so I'll have the secretary let you know if it's no problem.››

‹‹ No problem, she'll let us know,›› we agreed in unison.

‹‹ If you don't have any questions for me, we might as well dissolve the meeting...››

‹‹ Actually, I have one, if it's not too much trouble.››

‹‹ Go ahead, I'll be glad to answer it.››

‹‹ Thank you. In case, I'm just making a hypothesis... in case I don't agree with what you propose, what will happen?››

‹‹ You'll have to get a lawyer!››

Redemption days

I left that place of expensive pain first, while she lingered with the lawyer. That question must have thrown them off: first I had declared myself willing to settle and then... it almost seemed as if I wanted to say:' Hey guys! It was a joke! I'll fight to the bitter end with the help of my highly paid lawyer, and I'll even take away your lace panties! I would have left them to cook in their broth, for fun. Not only that, but I waited in front of the building's entrance. I knew it was a stupid move, but I wanted to talk to her alone. I had in my hands the file with her requests, and while waiting I read a few lines, so I didn't notice immediately that she had left. Furthermore, I saw that she was heading towards a car parked a short distance from the entrance and I called her loudly, but she accelerated her pace, without glancing at me, got into the car and disappeared, leaving behind only the exhaust fumes.

The sky had clouded over worryingly, I had to move too if I didn't want to risk getting a lot of water. The cabs whizzing down the street were all busy, so I opted for the subway. I was going to get off a few stops early for a visit to the old ED for a quick steak, rain is damned and so was she, not to mention I'd get to admire that lovely waitress and her inviting little balcony... No. No ED. I decided on a home-cooked dinner, so I was going to stop and shop. The subway was fast, but the cars were filling up at every stop, and I was starting to feel like I was inside a sardine can. I looked at the people around me and noticed, more and more, beings unworthy of living in the United States, inferior people, leeches living off the backs of honest white American citizens. They occupied the best jobs, taking them away from our young people, and in the worst cases, they devoted themselves to illegal activities such as drug dealing (sold to our young people) and prostitution, not to mention the shootings in the streets and the extortion racket... all evils imported from them. All of a sudden, a filthy nigger with a monkey face came so close to me that I could smell his revolting animal odor! I had to stop myself from vomiting inside the carriage! From the cut of the suit he was wearing, he must have earned a lot of money, and maybe he was occupying a prestigious position in some company (even in mine I used to meet many), stolen from some young, willing, and white man! What anger! Ever since one of them had been elected to the highest office in the nation, these monkeys thought they could do the best and the worst, but soon it would all be over, and they would be sent back to their bastard African continent to dance naked around the fire and pray to who knows what demonic stone idol. Thank goodness that it was just a little while away, one more stop and I would be rid of them and in particular of my 'neighbor'. The contact with that undeveloped monkey gave me hives... and his

Redemption days

smell... I couldn't stand it anymore. Even if he took a bath inside a tub filled with a very expensive perfume, he wouldn't lose that sick body odor. I was certain of it. The subway finally reached my stop and pushing my way through the crowd, I took the escape route, and once on the surface... I was able to breathe in the air filled with the sour smell of rain. Free at last! The clouds had cleared. Now the storm had passed, and I was going to walk the last stretch between now and my destination without the worry of being caught in the rain. I went in and grabbed one of the classic hand baskets for small purchases and began to browse through the various departments looking for the products I needed. I grabbed vegetables, meat, bread, beer (couldn't miss it), some fruit, a few bottles of wine, and a stash of various salty snacks. I placed my groceries on top of the conveyor belt, and as I watched the saleswoman's movements as she passed the individual items over the optical reader, I marveled at the countless differences between my groceries and Lorelain's.

‹‹ Envelope, sir?››

‹‹ Yes, thank you.››

‹‹ That will be 35.80. Cash or card?››

‹‹ Cash›› and handed her a 50 bill.

‹‹ Here's your change, thank you and goodbye.››

‹‹ Thank you and good night.››

Once home, I sorted out the groceries and then dealt with the remains of the closet still scattered around the room. I hoped it wasn't on the list of items he wanted, otherwise, 'I'm so sorry but your favorite closet is blown to smithereens! Nothing personal, though...', I would have found a better excuse than that. I didn't eat all the steak I had prepared for dinner, so I finished the whole bottle of beer, but I saved the bottle of wine, I needed it for the meeting with James. I began to read the lawyer's memo that decreed the end of my marriage to Lorelain. From what I read, she had not been too harsh towards me, on the contrary, her economic demands were human. She even declared herself willing to sell me her share of the house if I expressed the will to live there again (usually it is the husband who abandons the house in favor of his wife). Otherwise, the house would be sold, and we would each get our share of the money. Up to that point I hadn't found anything to object to about the requests, but I was getting tired (besides the cans of beer), so I decided to go and rest and left the file on the couch, ready for another reading the next morning, and I thought maybe I would do well to show it to a lawyer. Trusting is good, not trusting is better, especially with 'postage stamp' style clauses. The ones that leave you broke!

Redemption days

Finally, the weekend! Two days dedicated to absolute rest. Too much stress accumulated in those last days. Then on Sunday I would have met James and relaxed in his company. But I had to think about today. So after preparing myself, I decided to have breakfast in a coffee shop to start the day in the best way possible. From the window of the chosen place, I could see the whole world like in a movie... and I noticed several people who were dedicated to the ancient New York art of jogging and seeing them happily jogging, sweaty and tired inside their ultra-light and comfortable suits I remembered what my ex told me: "Dear you should do some exercise, you're putting on too many pounds, and it's certainly not healthy" I remembered that I had promised her that I would start jogging. But I always found an excuse to put off that fateful first day, so days turned into weeks and weeks into months... and I never started jogging. Even my gym membership didn't bring the desired results. After a week and then the total abandonment, at that point I realized that I was not suitable for the sport practiced in the first person, I could only be a spectator. Inside the club, you could admire all kinds of urban species that populated the city: someone was reading the newspaper sipping his drink, others had brought along the I-POD and, between a bite and a drink, surfing the net and me? Newspaper, a hot cappuccino garnished with a splash of chocolate, a dollop of whipped cream and to finish two dark chocolate chip muffins. Hearty breakfast! I shouldn't have given in to those delicious temptations, I had been getting a little heavier lately (also due to the alcohol I had been consuming in the last few days) but an extra pound certainly wouldn't have led to my death that day. I wanted to enjoy that morning pleasantly, to forget at least for those minutes my messes, the association, the bastard who had destroyed my friend's life, the divorce, and all the messes that plagued the world. Those minutes were for yours truly and that was it, the rest of the world would be left out of the diner window.

Sunday, finally Sunday. I was in front of the stove trying to prepare something edible for my guest. I had gotten up early that morning and went right to work cleaning up the whole house and seeing what condition it was in, I finally had to take a shower to clean myself up!

James arrived at the perfect time, I had just enough time to set the table and the last dish I was going to serve. My guest showed up with a bottle of red wine that I immediately opened to get some air, so he could fully taste the strong flavor during the lunch. In the meantime, I made him sit down in the living room and while waiting to sit down at the table, I offered him some appetizers accompanied by a can of beer. Frozen of course. I saw him standing in front of the shelf where there were still photos of the happy times and I called him to hand him the beer. He turned to me, took the can, and pointed to a photo in a simple frame with floral patterns.

‹‹ Beautiful, isn't it?››

‹‹ Just beautiful, yes...››. The picture of the famous field trip. We drank our beers while munching on pretzels.

‹‹ Lunch will be on the table in a few minutes. Don't expect anything fancy but don't worry, it's all edible stuff.››

‹‹ No problem, I'm a good eater.››

‹‹ Even for per-packaged meals?››

Redemption days

‹‹ Let's say yes, occasionally I use them too when I don't feel like putting myself on the stove.››

‹‹ Do you know how to cook?››

‹‹ Let's say that I can cook and until today, I have not killed anyone... now that I think about it, I could have helped you cook, I would have been pleased››

‹‹ I thank you for the offer but relax, even I haven't killed yet with the food I cook!›› and we laughed heartily.

The ice had melted again. We talked for another two minutes when I heard the microwave timer alerting us that lunch was finally ready. The roast was passable, though slightly stodgy, while the linguine with sauce came out eatable, though perhaps the only decent thing on the table was James' wine that went down like water. It took several minutes before our minds came out from the alcoholic fog that had enveloped them. After lunch, James explained to me the reason he had wanted to meet me at the club, the night he disappeared. He wasn't direct and took it in stride.

‹‹ When I first came to this city, I knew no one. Loneliness is a big, ugly beast. Little by little I managed to get out of the safe enclosure that I had created for myself to devote myself to exploring the world around me. Eventually, I managed to make a few acquaintances, turning some of them into true friendships, which made life in the city less burdensome for me››. His voice had a slight tremble. That boy had to take a big weight off his soul, and maybe the time had come. ‹‹ In every home, even in yours, you can find pictures of family members on special occasions... unfortunately this is not the case for me. I had to run away and take refuge here several years ago, cutting off any kind of relationship with my family.›› He seemed to be getting nervous or afraid. Maybe he was touching a nerve in his existence, a nerve that he had kept hidden for a long time in the depths of his mind. Hidden from all the people around him, and perhaps even from himself. He didn't want to continue to suffer.

‹‹ If it hurts you to talk about it... don't worry. You don't have to do that right now.››

‹‹ Don't worry... I think the time has come to talk about my life to saving someone very dear to me››.

‹‹ If that's what you want, but who is in danger?››

‹‹ I knew I could count on you, but to understand the whole story I have to talk about myself and my experience. I always gave my best in school, as I did in sports, church, and within the community. I never cut corners with anyone. One day I decided to share my homosexuality with my family... I thought the time was right to open up to them...››.

Redemption days

At that word I had a jolt of anger that I stifled before it exploded with impetus. I tried to remain calm but my face betrayed that intention. I should have kicked him out of the house, kicking his faggoty broken ass, but I don't know how, I held back. He got defensive, he understood the situation but continued to speak: « A lightning bolt in the sky... I know... I apologize, but you have to let me finish... a person's life is at stake... Then if you want, you can decide whether to help me or send me to fuck off. One chance... that's all I ask of you...». I gave him that goddamn chance, then I'd let it out.

‹‹ I won't make you lose any more time. I organized everything down to the smallest detail and in the days before the coming-out, I visualized in my mind every possible scenario and the possible reactions of my parents, especially my father. I didn't choose a particular evening. Just before starting dinner, I stood up and announced to all of them that I wanted to speak to them from the heart and when I saw that I had attracted their attention, I began to open up. Unfortunately, they did not let me finish. The reactions were the most desperate and convulsive. My mother burst into tears, declaring between sobs that she would have preferred a drugged or thieving son rather than an abomination against nature. She left the dining room covering her face with her hands, followed closely by my sister and my four-year-old brother, who was terrified by the sight of my father's angry attack on me. He heavily insulted me and in a fierce rage lashed out at me, brandishing a knife. He wouldn't stop insulting me... I dodged the blade and at that point, I decided to defend myself. I had to disarm him, it was painful, but I locked his wrist and slammed him against the wall to get him to loosen his grip. I screamed at him that I was still his son, his blood... and when he dropped the knife on the ground, I pushed him away from me, and he almost fell. Not giving up, he took to throwing everything on top of the table at me. Plates. Glasses. Cutlery. Everything. And always insulting me heavily. Finally, with tears in his eyes, he gave up and left. I remained alone in the room that had taken on the appearance of a battlefield. Pieces of glass scattered all over the floor, not to mention the remains of the dinner. What a mess! I could not resist the tears and cry in despair. Going upstairs, I went to my room... I stopped in front of their room for a few moments, trying to pick up some noise that could help me, but nothing. I thought that the next day I could somehow repair the

Redemption days

damage caused in the dining room and everything would be fine. The night always brought advice, and in the end, I fell asleep through my tears. A few hours before dawn, some men burst into the room and blocked me in, and drugged me with a strong dose of sedatives. In the late afternoon, I awoke in a hospital bed. Sterile, cold room, and alone. A single room, sparsely furnished. A bed, a bedside table, and a closet in which I found some clothes and a uniform that I should have worn in there. A barred window was my only link to the outside world. Contact with people from outside the center was strictly forbidden and even contact with family members, and surveillance was tight, I realized in the following days. Every day was marked by the many loudspeakers placed in every corner of the center announcing the various general appointments that each of us had to undergo, as well as the individual sessions, different for each of us. Time had lost its meaning in that place and my parents came to the center to bring me some spare clothes, but unfortunately, they did not want to meet me. The last time I saw them...was that very evening. The doctors, if they could be defined as such, reassured me that once healed I would be taken back into the bosom of my family nucleus but that, before that day, I would have to cut off all relations with the foreign world. Only in this way, I would be healed».

Until that moment, James had not stopped narrating, with a veil of sadness obscuring his face. My patience was running out. I would have waited a few more minutes and then finished or not, I would have unceremoniously thrown him out.

The therapy consisted of brainwashing. We were inundated with images of happy traditional families, told that each of us was straight and that we had embraced the so-called 'gay culture' during a period of disbandment. Ridiculous theories with no scientific basis. There was no shortage of corporal punishment, either. At least three times a week, we were beaten unceremoniously by the nurses, and other times we were ordered to undress and enter the showers where they dumped liters and liters of ice-cold water, with a powerful pump. If you were not careful, you risked falling to the ground, so powerful was the jet. According to them, these treatments served to cool our impure thoughts... then we had our usual meeting with the specialist, during which we were put under examination to test our progress. We were not allowed to socialize with the other 'guests' of the center, perhaps they were afraid that we would mate like hedgehogs, but with a few little tricks, you could manage to make friends. Little by little, I managed to make friends with a boy who was only fifteen years old, locked up by his family. We took courage from each other, but unfortunately, Steve was on the long road to self-destruction. Eventually, they had to lock him up in an isolation room, where he was monitored every four hours by the nurse on duty. Four days later, he was found dead in his cell. He had taken his own life, cutting his wrists with a piece of glass. I don't know how he managed to retrieve that rudimentary weapon, but he made his escape from that hell is the only way his desperation had conceived in those cursed nights. It wasn't the first suicide that took place within those walls, and it certainly wouldn't be the last. After his death, a book I had lent him some time ago was returned to me and inside it, I found a note in which he begged me to resist and find a way out and not to be angry with him, he would always be by my side and thanked me for everything I had done

Redemption days

for him since we met. He considered me as a big brother, ready to help him and defend him... unfortunately, I couldn't save him! After five months spent in that hell, one day I hid inside the sacks of dirty laundry that were picked up every Wednesday by the trucks of a specialized company, and so I managed to escape. Once out of that lager, I had to give myself to the bush and with the help of some voluntary associations, I changed state and city and came here, destroying all the bridges that put me...».

I jumped up and with dexterity, I took him by the shirt and staring him in the eyes I said in a firm voice: « Time's up. Now the little shit fag, if he goes with his legs, otherwise...» and I dragged him by weight towards the door. He didn't resist but resumed talking, trying to convince me to desist and allow him to finish the story. He begged me to stop, but that traitor was playing with fire and was in danger of burning himself alive! I threw him out of the apartment and closed the door in his face, telling him to disappear forever from my life. At that point, he started pounding his fists hard against the door, begging me to help him save him... save Arthur! His Arthur! That name had made me wince, and I let him back into the house.

‹‹ Are you talking about Arthur? John's son? My friend?›› I asked, and he nodded his head in the affirmative. I couldn't believe that I was looking at myself, the bastard who had ruined John and his family. Furthermore, I could have taught him the lesson he deserved instantly, but I held back, John would be the one to carry out the revenge, and so I decided to let him talk further. A stroke of luck that I would have to play to my strengths. After calming down, James told the rest of his story to Arthur. The two of them met through the internet on one of those filthy sites for people like him, and after a short while decided to meet in person. Arthur was not even 17 years old, he had only a few months ago become aware of his 'so-called' sexual orientation and took his first steps inside that filthy abnormal world of queers. She had convinced him that all that world was normal and beautiful, and poor Arthur had fallen into that damned trap, other than love... she had led him astray in a period of difficulty, of this, there was no doubt. In the early days they met in secret, away from prying eyes, they avoided shopping malls, main streets, and well-known places, but not James' apartment. He told me that when he had to stay at his place, Arthur told his parents that he was staying at a friend's or schoolmate's house and I didn't even dare to think about what had happened inside that apartment... what an abomination! I had to stay calm, I couldn't explode, I couldn't blow everything up.

Redemption days

After a night spent at his house, Arthur decided to reveal their love to everyone, he didn't want to live it secretly anymore, but James tried to dissuade him, according to him the moment hadn't come and convinced him to give up right in the headquarters of their association (the day John found out the truth about his son!) and from that evening he couldn't get in touch with Arthur, until the day he learned of his forced hospitalization in a specialized clinic. He didn't know what to do and asked the association for help, and then he remembered that during a conversation with Arthur, he found out that I was a friend of his father's, and so he decided to ask me for help to convince the latter to withdraw Arthur from that lager before it was too late. I promised him that I would do everything in my power to convince John to withdraw Arthur from the clinic to try to stall and set the record straight. He thanked me, and as he left the house I told him I would be in touch, I couldn't accept everything about that world, but his words had made me question some of my ideas. I gave him my word but made him promise to keep the secret for the time being. No one had to know, especially the members of his association. I heartened him by assuring him that before long he would be able to embrace his love again, and I apologized to him for my violent reaction earlier... I told him that perhaps the stress accumulated in that last period had made me lose my mind. Fortunately, he understood my mistakes and thanked me further for my willingness to help him save Arthur.

That same night I made the phone call that would resolve the situation. Solved in my way. I understood everything James had been through, but John had lost so much more. Not to mention that John was my friend and James was my subordinate.

A car parked at night near a little-used alley stood waiting. A second car was placed a short distance from the first. The time for action had not yet come. A shadow was approaching the entrance of the alley, and at that point two men got out of the first car and rushed at the shadow, blocking it and dragging it inside the alley. After a few minutes, the members of the second car got out and went inside the alley to find themselves in front of the shadow, immobilized and unconscious, hands and feet tied to a wire mesh and his mouth well plugged. In the meantime, John and I arrived. That alley reeked of urine (an open-air latrine), dark and fetid beyond belief, the area had little traffic, but just in case, we had procured balaclavas that completely covered his face.

Seeing him unconscious, tied to that net, his head bowed to one side, his face swollen from the blows taken during the fight, and that wire as handcuffs gave me a sense of anguish, but I could not forget that I was facing the bastard who had led little Arthur astray. I wasn't going to interfere. I had done my part, now I just had to enjoy the show, in the company of the others. John's eyes shone with intense and dark light. John approached the creature and slapped it heavily and repeatedly to make it come to its senses, he didn't want to hit it when it was unconscious. He wanted to face him face to tell him everything he thought about him and all the harm he had caused to his family.

‹‹ Wake up little princess! Little princess? Wake up...you must entertain us...››.

Redemption days

James answered with some unintelligible mumbling but when he fully recovered, his first words were: ‹‹ Who...who...are...you...what do you want?››.

He tried to free his wrists but couldn't, he hadn't fully processed the situation yet, but he understood that he was in trouble. In the meantime, I remained in the shadows to observe the evolution of the situation.

‹‹ It doesn't matter who we are. You should worry about something else, you perverted little whore!›› and she punched him in the stomach, making him let out a muffled cry of pain.

‹‹ Poor thing! I bet you want to know the reason for this treatment, don't you?›› asked John with a grin that distorted his face.

James asked him again who he was and took a flurry of punches between his stomach and face. He wanted to play like a cat with a mouse, John was having fun. Punch to the stomach! Punch to the face! A well-placed kick to the testicles! The boy didn't even have time to scream in pain. He was out of breath. Slaps, spits, and insults as a frame for his sadistic game. The accomplice, who acted as a lookout at the entrance of the alley, was on the alert in case some curious person wanted to spoil the party. The tension of being discovered increased John's sadism towards James. By now, the boy was held up only by his restraints, tied to the net. He no longer reacted to the blows that were inflicted. At one point, I caught a glimpse of his face completely swollen, and I decided to take my friend aside to talk to him. I grabbed him by the arm and dragged him a few feet away from his toy to try to put a stop to his destructive fury.

‹‹ What the fuck do you want?›› growled the bloodthirsty beast.

‹‹ You have to stop this! That one already got his punishment, and you got your revenge!››

‹‹ We're just at the beginning, what do you think? Did you let that dirty little whore suck you off?››

Redemption days

‹‹ Don't talk bullshit! Don't you realize you've lost your mind?››. Nothing! Now John was out of the world. In a world of his own, full of hate and rancor towards the boy. He was no longer thinking. The light that crossed his eyes sent shivers down his spine. His anger had yet to be fulfilled to give vent to his darker side. What was supposed to be a simple 'lesson' was turning into torture? We had carried out much bloodier and stronger actions than that one, where even someone had died, but they were always actions coordinated by the association. None of us, since we had joined the organization, had taken personal actions in order not to risk trouble with the authorities. John was taking his revenge through the association, and he certainly wouldn't stop until James took his last breath. In that case, the safety of all of us would have been seriously jeopardized, but John didn't realize it and my speech had only increased his fury. He left me to go towards James who was still unconscious, and he had one of his teammates pass him the baseball bat and with a tone between serious and cold, he said: ‹‹ Let's have fun!››.

He struck him in several places with force and blind determination. The other no longer made a sound. The sounds of bones breaking under the blows of the bat echoed sinisterly. James seemed narcotized. A ligature snapped and the body half slumped. John still hadn't stopped, alternating between blows from the bat and kicks to his private parts. Suddenly he aimed at the arm still tied to the metal net and with a sharp blow he broke it. He didn't stop there. He continued to hit that arm repeatedly as if he wanted to reduce it to dust. At that point I ventured against him in an attempt to block him, the matter had gone beyond even for me. Unfortunately, John did not want to stop and tried to hit me with the bat. I avoided the blow by just an inch. He was railing against me, against the other members present, against James, and everything else in the world. The man had completely lost his mind. Fortunately, the other member also tried to disarm him, he too had realized that the situation had degenerated. Only after half an hour did we manage to calm him down and get him away from his prey, who was now dying. I asked the two of them to take John out of the alley and to wait for me there, I would have reached them immediately. John grunted something incomprehensible, but the two guards marked him tightly, and finally, he let them escort him to the exit. In the alleyway, it was me and the former boy. I freed him from his last chain and with the utmost caution, I placed him completely on the ground. I could hardly recognize him. His deformed face was swollen and bruised. Blood clotted all over his body. His clothes were tattered and filthy. Looking at him in that state, I was assailed by doubts about that punitive action. I had condemned him to death by serving him on a silver platter to his tormentor. After all, he had confided in me, he had opened his heart to ask me for help... he had trusted me and I had betrayed him... No! Damn it! It wasn't my fault he was in that

Redemption days

state! He was asking for it! Fuck him! He deserved that punishment, the right one for that kind of being against nature. I left him in the alley, dying and unconscious. I abandoned him to his fate. Furthermore, I erased from my mind those ridiculous second thoughts and I left, turning my back on him. No remorse. They had to suffer the pains of hell on this earth as an appetizer to what they would suffer for eternity for their abominable behavior.

Life resumed its usual rhythms, even John's. From that evening on, no one mentioned that episode again, but sometimes I saw that strange light appear in John's gaze. I signed contracts, resolutions, and orders, and attended meetings, but I avoided my colleagues and especially in his empty office. Strange normality. Only four days later I was blocked in the underground parking lot of the office by Ellen, a colleague with whom I had exchanged the usual greetings, a few working directives, and nothing more. That evening, she wanted to talk to me, going so far about knock on the window of my car insistently. I reluctantly lowered the window and greeted her, warning her that I was in a hurry and suggesting that we postpone the meeting until the next day (surely it was work-related) but she didn't give in: «It's about James!» I blanched at the mention of that name. I didn't say anything. Furthermore, I just stared at her.

«Is this about the guy who interned with you...the new hire? Remember?»
«I remember.»

I stared into her eyes but couldn't see them, I could see darkness. She took to telling the latest news about James. A police patrol, on night duty, had received several reports of strange movements of people in a suburban alley, an area known to the authorities as a crossroads of shady business including drug dealing and prostitution. Patrol 45 responded to the call and went to the place but found nothing strange, so they decided to enter the alley to check and at that point, they found themselves in front of a dead body. Perhaps in that alley, there had been a settling of scores between rival gangs or a customer who had not paid his debt with his personal 'pusher'. One of the agents approached the corpse, while his companion illuminated the surroundings to flush out any intruder, both weapons in his fist. He bent over him and, to his surprise, noticed that he was still breathing, albeit weakly. They wasted no time and called an ambulance. James was rushed to Saint Mary's Hospital in extremely poor condition. The paramedics didn't think he would make it there alive, but the boy had a strong character and a strong will to live. Broken bones, head trauma, broken ribs, a crushed spleen and liver, hematomas all over his body, not to mention all the blood he had lost. He was given several blood transfusions, three bags, just to get his values back within the limits. He underwent many emergency surgeries and was kept in a medically induced coma to prevent further complications. The agents were still investigating the incident, looking for possible witnesses, they were leaning towards a robbery gone wrong. Before leaving the alley I had taken his wallet and valuables, fortunately, I had worn latex gloves to avoid leaving fingerprints and from what I could hear, I had done a great job of misdirection. After the recognition, the authorities notified his family, but nobody showed up: they didn't want to have anything more to do with the boy, for them, he was dead

Redemption days

various years ago. The news of the attack had reached our director a few hours earlier, and within minutes it was on everyone's lips. Ellen thought about informing me but, if she had known the truth about that tragedy, she would have surely killed me with her own hands, because she secretly had a crush on the boy. When she had finished her report, I put on the saddest face in my repertoire, spoke a few sentences, and said goodbye. If I had stayed a few more minutes in her presence, I might have exploded and spilled the beans... and found myself in a cold cell in two seconds.

That same night, the remorse grew stronger and did not leave me until the first light of day. I even thought of going to the hospital the next morning to see him, to find out about his condition, but I didn't do it. Neither that morning nor the next. Thanksgiving came too quickly and unexpectedly, as did the invitation to spend it at John's house, in the company of his family. I gladly accepted. I had no desire to be alone. Surely my ex-wife would not invite me to spend it with her, and so in the morning, I went to John's house with a good bottle of wine. That Thanksgiving would have been special for John his son would have been there as well, he had been discharged from the clinic just two days before. The doctors had been true to their word, not to mention that the pest had been put out of action, so there was no danger of relapse. I would not be the only one invited to that lunch, between John's parents, his sister, and brother-in-law with their respective families, there would be eleven of us. All gathered around the well-laid table, in the center a pretty (according to taste) plastic centerpiece in the shape of a turkey dressed as a pilgrim and at the sides two cornucopias, also plastic and 'Made in China'.

After the customary greetings to those present, I took John by the arm and, with a trivial excuse, led him out into the garden for a brief exchange, far from prying ears. I noticed that he was setting up a small swing in the center of the garden next to a square filled with sand. Old John was setting up a recreational area for the newcomer.

‹‹ I see you've taken up construction.››
‹‹ It's all about the little things. I don't want to be unprepared, in certain situations it's better to get ahead of the game. Don't you think so?›› and he smiled.
‹‹ You know he's dying?››

His face darkened as he heard this, and his smile faded into a grimace of hatred. In his eyes, no sign of repentance or remorse, but only that strange light. As far as he was concerned, the case was closed that very night, but not for me.

‹‹ A colleague of mine, a few days ago, alerted me to the incident and invited me to go to him at the hospital...››
‹‹ Did you go there?››
‹‹ No... but I thought about it a lot››.
‹‹ You're not going soft on me, I hope? The future head of the organization must be of steel and devoid of feelings, don't you agree?››
‹‹ I do agree. Just...››
‹‹ Now let's go back in. The topic is closed! I mean, closed forever!››.

Redemption days

The one who answered me was no longer the friend I knew. He had tasted the blood of his intended victim, and the primordial taste of inflicting pain on another human being had intoxicated him to the point of making him feel untouchable. Each of us has his dark half, hidden in some corner of the mind, ready to take over in certain situations, and for John, it was the misfortune that happened to his son to turn him into a bloodthirsty beast.

‹‹ Arthur?›› I asked before he crossed the threshold of the house. At that point, he turned in my direction and in a cheerful manner gave me a pat on the back then with a soft and calm tone told me: ‹‹ Everything is fine. He's fine, and you can see that with your own eyes. He certainly won't have any relapse. Now let's go inside, I hear that all the other guests have arrived.››.

We gathered in the living room for a small aperitif while discussing this and that. I had known my friend's parents for many years, while with the others I had only had sporadic meetings and a few exchanges of greetings. All of a sudden, Mary, flanked by her mother-in-law and sisters-in-law, invited everyone to take their seats as lunch would soon be served. Arthur came down at that moment and after a round of greetings took his place at the table. He was not affectionate, he limited himself to a simple 'hello' and a few handshakes with some kisses on the cheeks, nothing more. As far as I remember, he had never been an expansive guy, not even before his hospitalization, but his cold and absent look made me feel uncomfortable. During lunch, the discussions, anecdotes, and memories were wasted. After the first course, the party took off. That festive, familial harmony made me a little wistful. I was reminded of past holidays spent with my wife and her relatives, although to be honest, I had never endured them more I was holding out for my beloved and only for her. Lorelain had a magic touch in the kitchen and how she prepared the chestnut stuffed turkey... a delicacy that made even those who didn't have them lick their lips, it was so good. Sadly, those times would not return, and I had to deal with it.

Redemption days

After that sumptuous meal, there was the usual Brown family tradition of reciting poems and songs performed by the youngest children to the "joy" of the adults present, sitting, and intent on digesting and trying not to sleep. The first to do without that show would have been the actors themselves, but the Browns' traditions did not allow for interruptions. The living room was set up for the play, which was divided into three parts, two poems and a song all on the theme of Thanksgiving performed by John's grandchildren. Two rows of chairs, the sofa was removed at the last moment (perhaps it was too conducive to sleep) but two armchairs remained for the elderly parents.

First performance: little girl, 6 years old, elegant red dress with matching shoes. Short poem. Applause from all present except Arthur.

Second performance: Boy, 9 years old, pants, white shirt with bow tie, and second poem. Unfortunately, the little boy froze in a few places, turning bright red in the face from excitement but it was all resolved with a little help from his mother.

Applause from everyone in attendance except Arthur.

Third performance: Little girl, 8 years old, soberly dressed as a little woman. A song about the first thanksgiving celebrated by the pilgrims. Applause from all present, except Arthur.

At that point we were about to get up from our chairs to end the evening among us adults and leave the kids to play a little among themselves when: ‹‹ My interpretation is missing, please return to your seats, thank you all››.

All of us were stunned by that announcement. Arthur, who had not spoken for all that time, begged us to sit down again to watch his mysterious and unexpected performance. John, who was bursting with joy, motioned us to take our seats, and then gave the go-ahead to his eldest son, who had already settled down in front of the house audience. The show could begin.

‹‹ I will tell you a story. Human beings try in every way to love and be reciprocated by their loved ones. We need someone's affection to get by in this crazy and violent modern world. However, not everyone is lucky enough to find it, some people are satisfied with the first person who reciprocates with an ephemeral and sterile feeling, others still... can not love... not because they do not have feelings, quite the opposite. Unfortunately, they are terrified of loving in the light of day, of shouting it out to the whole world, to their families, to their friends... to the entire bigoted society... because they are terrified that no one will be able to fully understand their love››.

Redemption days

John suddenly turned white as his wife began to show signs of fright. The other relatives present were trying to understand his strange speech when suddenly John got up from his chair and shouted at his son to shut up, since he didn't know what he was saying, and ordered him to go to his room. He made the move to walk up to him to forcibly grab him to drag him away from the living room, but he froze a few steps away and stepped aside, allowing us a glimpse of a gun. Arthur was armed with his father's gun, which he had kept hidden throughout lunch, perhaps behind his back. He intimated to his father to sit back down and turned to all of us and said that we had to stay calm. John didn't let him repeat it twice, and neither did we. He took a long breath and resumed speaking: "Unfortunately, you interrupted our conversation and this is a sign of bad manners. I bet you've already called 911 on your cell phones... so I'll have to go with the short version!" and laughed with gusto.

An evil taste.

‹‹ Arthur... my son... put the gun down... please!››

‹‹ Shut up! I am not your son! You are not my mother! Shut up!›› he yelled, pointing the gun in her face. The woman choked back a scream of terror. None of us moved a single muscle for fear of her reaction, while the children clutched terrified and crying at their parents, who shielded them with their bodies. The boy seemed lucid and determined in his display of strength and was not completely unfamiliar with firearms he was an expert marksman. His father had taken him shooting with him in the open country since he was a child, and once they had gone to the neighboring state to attend a gun show, where they could try out all kinds of firearms, from ordinary pistols to those used by the army, and they had both had a lot of fun. The passion he had passed on to his son was now backfiring on him. The kidnapper ordered the older boy to take the other two into the garden and stay there, and they, terrified, obeyed, leaving the room in tears.

‹‹ I tell you not to be heroes. I have enough bullets for all of you and I also have a very good aim, so you do it. Now listen to me in silence because the first one who will allow himself to interrupt me will find his mouth full of lead!›› and he made "shhh" bringing the barrel of the gun to his nose.

‹‹ I finally found a person who loved me for who I was. A unique person who made me feel special... my boyfriend... yeah you heard me right... I said, boyfriend! I LOVED A GUY LIKE ME!›› screamed angrily.

John plugged his ears, so he wouldn't hear him say those words, and yelled forcefully.

‹‹ NO! MY SON IS NOT ONE OF THOSE... HE'S NOT AN ABOMINATION AGAINST NATURE... NOT YOU... YOU'RE CURED!››.

Redemption days

BANG! Ahhhhh!

‹‹ Unclean being?››

I saw my friend fall to the floor screaming in pain as he held his wounded leg with his hands, from which a lot of blood was pouring out. The bullet must have lodged in the bone because I didn't see it come out. When the shot rang out, everyone in the room took their escape route, amidst screams and cries of terror. In the hall, there were four of us left. Arthur the Executioner, Mary the Mad, John the Dying, and me, the Judas. He had calculated everything down to the tiniest detail and had achieved his aim, which was to keep those responsible for his hell under fire. In the distance, the police sirens could be heard echoing, it was now a matter of minutes.

In that damned clinic where you locked me up, I suffered like never before! Every night, I cried and tried to figure out what was wrong with me that caused me so much pain. I thought and thought and in the end, I understood that there was nothing wrong with me the real problem was you and those crazy people who called themselves doctors! In the end, I realized that if I wanted to come out of that godforsaken place sane, I would have to behave the way they wanted me to. You see dear my daddy...I acted so well that they were convinced of my recovery and let me out early!' The sirens stopped screaming, a clear signal that the patrol cars had arrived in front of the house and that the policemen were cordoning off the area with the classic yellow tape, trying to drive away from the first escapees and the usual onlookers who had already gathered in front.

‹‹ My goal was just to get home and escape with my love... but nothing! It would have been easier for all of you if we had succeeded in the escape, but something went wrong. We had decided everything, the place of the appointment and even the city where we would be reborn, unfortunately, James didn't show up. The people at the clinic trusted me so much that they gave me a phone call... and I called him to explain the whole thing and my escape plan, which he approved as an extreme gesture of salvation. I knew when I was going to be discharged, so we decided to meet the next day at the mall, but he didn't show up. I thought he was having second thoughts but... no... he loved me too much... in the end, I went home, through my bedroom window. I was resigning myself when...›› he took a breath and wiped away the tears that were streaming down his face ‹‹ I learned from some mutual friends that James was dying in the hospital because of a violent beating that had taken place the night before our date. He even asked his superior, whom he trusted like a father, to intercede for the two of us with you... it was a friend of yours who betrayed him! Earlier he had assured him that he would do what he could, but instead, that dirty corrupt man immediately ran to warn you.›› and he gave me a look of hatred.

‹‹ We both know very well that you organized the ambush with the complicity of your crazy friend! Tell me... did you enjoy beating the shit out of him? Did it make you feel like a man? Tell me ... BASTARD! TELL ME TO MY FACE THAT YOU TOOK PLEASURE IN BEATING YOUR SON'S BOYFRIEND! TELL ME!››

Redemption days

John did not accept the provocation. The police ultimatum had expired. Just a few more minutes and they would break in.

‹‹ Coward! You don't answer... you're right, I also went to see him in the hospital, and seeing him attached to those machines made me angry but what destroyed me the most knew that whoever had reduced him to that vegetative state was my own father.›› His hands were shaking with anger, but he didn't lose control.

‹‹ We also made love... it sucks for you, doesn't it? I liked it very much since we loved each other! You destroyed our life... you destroyed our love... and for what? Simply out of ignorance and fear of the comments that your friends, relatives, neighbors, or strangers would have made if they had known that your firstborn son liked to take it up the ass! You heard me right... TAKE IT IN THE BUTT! Because you damn people reduce everything to that, you can't see the feelings and love that two people in the love of the same sex feel... no... you reduce it to just TAKE IT IN THE BUTT and that's it! Now look me in the eye... the two of you too... Don't you dare look away: no, I won't let you. You must look at your death sentence...››.

A sharp, powerful shot echoed through the living room. The second of that tragic, bloody afternoon. Arthur had carried out his revenge on those who had ruined his life and that of James. An indelible mark etched with the fire of eternal damnation, like a modern Cain! The boy lay on the cold floor, bathed in a pool of blood. Chunks of the brain had splattered on the walls of the fireplace and the room as blood continued to spill from the body, the smoking gun still clutched in his hands. The cops burst in and put an end to the family tragedy that had rocked a small suburban American neighborhood.

Mary had such a physical and mental breakdown that she had to be rushed to the hospital for a C-section. Unfortunately, the baby did not make it. The congenital malformation of the heart and the severe trauma caused her death.

The forensic agents had finished their investigations a few minutes before, so the body was placed inside a black bag and transported out of the crime scene. Questions upon questions from the authorities to reconstruct the events that occurred that day.

'How did he get the weapon?'

'Had he shown signs of intolerance before today?'

'Any clashes within the family?'

'Are you aware of the motive that drove him to that act?'

Redemption days

Our answers were vague, and eventually, they let us go, inviting us to remain available for further questions. By now, in front of the house, television vans and journalists could be seen, as well as the usual onlookers and neighbors. The press exploited the news for several weeks, filling the front pages of local newspapers, not to mention the television reports with countless interviews with relatives, victims, friends, or strangers, and psychologists who were wasted on talk shows to find the fuse that had triggered that tragedy. The finger was pointed at the possession of weapons in civilian homes, but when Arthur's homosexuality came to light, and it was known of his forced hospitalization in the clinic to treat him, public opinion split into two opposing factions until the news disappeared completely from the media.

On the day of the funeral in the cemetery, there weren't many people, many relatives avoided participating in the burial because they didn't want to hear any more of that ugly story or maybe of shame, but the dearest friends were present. Around the coffin, covered with flowers and with a simple wreath placed on the right side, we listened in perfect silence to the homily of the priest who handed over the tormented soul to the Lord. Matt, Jason, and I huddled around our friend, who was sitting in a wheelchair with his gaze lost in the void and his eyes swollen and red from too many tears shed. Few of his son's friends dared to offer condolences, but everyone huddled around his ex-wife and Arthur's mother, sitting a few seats away from us, wracked with grief at losing her only son. She threw some dirt over the coffin as it was lowered into the grave, but her sorrows were not over. The small white coffin was laid on the cold earth a few minutes later next to her older brother's grave. A family tragedy. John did not want to leave, he did not want to abandon his two sons, forcing us to remove him firmly from that place of sorrow. At the end of the funeral ceremony, I noticed Lorelain walking to her car and I tried to reach her to talk to her, I apologized to my friends and ran to her. Now it was no longer a secret, my divorce. I stopped her a few meters from the car and the reception was not the best. Cold and detached.

‹‹ Hello... How come you are also at the function?›› I said, trying to shake her hand to greet her, but she pretended not to see that gesture.

‹‹ I watched Arthur grow up, and I am very close to both Mary and Gill and I couldn't leave them at this moment of pain!››

‹‹ I understand completely. John and I are like brothers and I couldn't turn my back on him... given the tragic and unexpected end of his son and little girl››.

‹‹ Unexpected? Do you realize what you're saying?››

‹‹ Nobody expected him to commit suicide. None of us!››

‹‹ No one? It was you who caused all this! You and your damned comrades in the association, and especially John! You and no one else!››

‹‹ Don't you dare... damn it! You weren't there that damned afternoon, and you don't know how things went... He went crazy!››

Redemption days

‹‹ Crazy because of your intolerance! It was you who pulled the trigger of that gun, not Arthur! It was you! You have destroyed many lives, and you know it too!›› and he walked away. He had hit the mark. I didn't reply. I was the only one responsible and no one else, and that hurt.

In the meantime, the association was beginning the great maneuvers for the change at the top and according to the latest unofficial polls, I was in a clear advantage over my direct opponent, thanks to that punitive expedition. Somebody had leaked the fact, and it didn't matter that the family of an associate had been destroyed, after all, "James the greaser" was the only guilty party, and he got what he deserved. After all that had happened, I could have withdrawn from the competition and left the association as well, but my subconscious wanted to take over that seat and so it did. The outcome was overwhelming. My rival 'Mouse Face' did not digest the defeat (he lost with a gap of 350 votes!) and left the room in perfect "showgirl" style, followed by his tail of lackeys. The first to congratulate me was the outgoing president, then I was surrounded by other members who competed to shake my hand and congratulate me on my victory. The glasses were raised and the winner's speech began. Here's what they all expected: the speech of the new leader with the directives for the new course, which according to many would not be very different from those of the old leadership, unfortunately, I just thanked them for their support and ended with the classic wish for good work. From their faces, I could see that they didn't like it very much, but the old lion came to my rescue and calmed down: ‹‹ Friends! Brothers! I believe that I am the bearer of my successor's thoughts when I say that we must reduce discussions and increase real actions. Rest assured that when the time comes to act, he will be in the front line fighting side by side with each one of you for the success of our cause, that of the United States of America, and the entire white and Aryan world! White Power!››.

Redemption days

The applause was wasted... then our hymn echoed through the room, crowning it all with thanks to our country and God. The evening continued with alcohol, smoke, and fun.

‹‹ Let them have fun, meanwhile, you come with me, so you can finally take possession of your office››.

‹‹ Office?›› I asked.

‹‹ The boss's office, right?››

‹‹ No, look, it's no problem for me. You can keep it, don't worry!››

‹‹ Now you're the boss, so the control room is yours too››.

‹‹ OK, but you're always welcome››.

Once in the study, he took a seat in one of the two guest chairs, leaving the main one free. The handover had finally happened.

‹‹ What's bothering you?››

‹‹ Nothing›› I smiled or at least tried to smile.

‹‹ Nothing, I wouldn't say. Remember that now you run the show, and you must have a clear mind.

‹‹ You mustn't be seen as indecisive or hesitant in front of the others, as you did a few minutes ago››.

‹‹ No uncertainties, I got caught up in the excitement of victory and that's all.

‹‹ So it had nothing to do with what happened on Thanksgiving?›› Exploratory question.

‹‹ Arthur's suicide is... not a pretty sight.››

‹‹ I agree with you, but I wouldn't want that episode to have corrupted you, given also your strange approach to the greaser. I would like to be sure of your loyalty to this association and its purpose because you are sitting in that chair because of my help. Don't you ever forget that!››.

I reassured him across the board.

That little speech had got me thinking. It almost seemed like a warning not to slip up. We gave each other a farewell handshake, and eventually, I was left alone to think.

I should have given the walls a coat of paint, they needed it. I checked the drawers of the desk: no documents, as empty as those in the filing cabinet. He had left nothing behind, and here I was thinking of checking out the association's famous archive if it ever existed! An archive in which all the names of the members of the association from its foundation up to the present day were to be recorded, including those who had left, but as I said, perhaps it was an urban legend, not even the police had managed to find it and... hell, none of us had ever had it in our hands or seen it apart from the old boss. From what was rumored, that archive had also served over the years as a weapon of blackmail to shut the mouths of outsiders; after all, the organization didn't allow chatterboxes. I could have removed that doubt by asking the old boss directly, but I wasn't sure if he had informed me of its existence.

‹‹ Now that you're the boss, you're making yourself wanted.››

Redemption days

Matt's voice brought me back from the world of thought I had fallen into. I waved him in and behind him, I caught a glimpse of Phil and greeted them warmly, finally two friendly faces.

‹‹ So... best wishes for the victory!›› said Matt all cheerful as he took his place on the chair, but Phil made a rather truthful and distressing statement: ‹‹ A victory paid dearly for!››.

He was right, that victory had taken a high toll that John paid dearly. Silence fell over us. Seeing the situation, Matt asked me for explanations about my meeting with the old boss, since they had glimpsed him coming out of the studio a few minutes ago with a dark and angry expression, so I told them about the meeting and the warning that I was there thanks to his interest and that I should not do my own thing and from their expressions, they made me understand that something was wrong.

‹‹ I don't understand his game. Resigning, calling a new election by backing you to win for a simple matter of facade? At the end of the day, he could have had Rat-Face elected, since he's only looking for prestige and that's all, and he would have done whatever he was told without much trouble. He is a 'Yes man' but not you››.

Matt's reasoning was right, even Phil was convinced, but why? Why? A question that was unlikely to be answered. Phil asked me about John's state of health and the details of that bloody afternoon, I wanted to back out, but then I began to tell the whole story and I didn't try to lighten my position. I would have accepted their judgment, whatever it had been. The party on the other side was slowly fading, now the voices were decreasing little by little, and many had begun to leave the building to go home or continue to celebrate in a 'private' form in some local of the city.

‹‹ Someone has used you for a perverse game!›› said Phil.

Knock. Knock.

‹‹ Come in!›› I said.

When you talk about the devil, horns come out...

‹‹ Excuse me, I didn't know that there was a restricted meeting››.
‹‹ No meeting, just a sports discussion. Can I help you?›› I did, spreading my arms behind my back, stretching slightly. A clear signal that he meant: "Too comfortable this chair and the power!".
‹‹ Nothing important, I just wanted to warn you that you are left alone in the association, so you close?››
‹‹ Thank you and don't worry, we will close. Just a few more minutes, and we'll leave too. Good evening››

Redemption days

‹‹ OK, good evening to you too›› and left us. That sudden visit of the old man, made us jump the flea to the nose, so we decided to continue the conversation in a nightclub.

At that hour the bar was not full, and we could discuss things quietly. By now the seed of suspicion had taken root in my mind, also thanks to the doubts of my two friends: why me and not someone else? My rival would have been fine, and we knew it, but he had chosen me. A strange and incomprehensible situation. I spoke about the secret archives (they also knew the story) and they had different opinions about the existence of this phantom volume where all the sensitive data of the association was locked up.

‹‹ No one has ever seen it in person, so in my opinion, it's an urban legend. Just to scare those without assholes!›› said Matt, swallowing some peanuts taken from a bowl placed on the table.
‹‹ Come on, even if nobody has seen it, it doesn't mean a prior that it doesn't exist. What do you think, Phil?››
‹‹ No one has seen it, so it doesn't exist!››
‹‹ You're stubborn, Matt!››.

When he got stubborn... Phil intervened with calm and biblical wisdom, managing to put us in agreement.

‹‹ Guys, I can tell you that in my opinion there are two lists. And don't look so surprised. Surely there is a public directory for internal use within the association›› Phil was right.

One public directory did exist, and I could see it for myself, but it only covered active members and that was it.

‹‹ The other, I believe, is well-kept in some safe and contains not only the names of present and current members, but also those who have passed and leftover time, but...››
‹‹ Excuse me Phil, but what is the point of having two separate lists? I don't see the point››

‹‹ Matt, the utility is obvious and simple. In the secret one, there are not only names but also other sensitive and personal information that can be used for various blackmails. So I don't think the old boss will ever let you see it.››
‹‹ Blackmail?›› said Matt, alarmed.
‹‹ Blackmail. Let's be honest at least with ourselves, our organization is not in the business of pious works, or am I wrong? I'm not wrong. The secret list is a kind of insurance against any chatterers and doesn't tell me you fall from the clouds››
‹‹ So somewhere there would be a file with my name on it with personal information?›› asked Matt. Phil simply nodded in the affirmative and finished drinking his beer. We were all being blackmailed without our knowledge. How could this relate to the travesty of my election and John's tragedy? I asked them.
‹‹ I don't know. I tell you with all my heart, this story stinks, and we could get burned,›› Matt said.

Redemption days

As Phil answered with another question, ‹‹ Did John unintentionally spite the old man with your help?››

‹‹ Do you think he wants to do me in? Neither John nor I have wronged the boss. We have always been loyal to him and the whole association, and you are witnesses to that...so I don't understand...››

‹‹ We know, but the one who had to end was John and not you.››

‹‹ Why John?›› asked Matt.

Why? Simple, because of Arthur's illness. A stain on the integrity of the association that had to be erased with blood. Now everything was taking shape in my mind and particularly in Phil's.

‹‹ John was eliminated and I was brought under control. I have to tell you, I don't like this situation at all. I consider it a low and treacherous and senseless blow››

‹‹ A trap set with all the trappings, and I feel that at this point none of us can consider ourselves safe from 'Rat Face'!››.

We remained silent. To tell you the truth, my suspicions had focused on the old man, and... 'Rat Face' hadn't even made the list. Phil at that point explained his theory: John had been the first to believe in my election and had spared no effort in the campaign. So by bashing John 'Rat Face' he wanted to bash yours truly, he had set it all up. The old boss, he had supported me anyway, and maybe he didn't know anything of what that bastard had done. But my doubts about the old man didn't leave me entirely. That night, an external phalanx came to life against that rat bastard, but we had to keep all our senses alert to avoid a counter-offensive on their part. Our main task would have been to recover the secret archive because in there we could have found some compromising information on the bastard... and perhaps the information on John's son's illness had been read on that damn archive. Of this I was certain. Perhaps some ex-members might have been aware of where that archive was kept, so we decided to retrieve the old lists of ex-members and have a nice informal chat with them. Those interviews would confirm or not the thesis of the existence of the archives. We left with a promise to avenge John and his family.

Redemption days

The work in the office seemed to increase more and more, while the interest in the story of James was waning day by day. People have a habit of forgetting tragedies too quickly, and James' story was no exception. In the relaxation room, I met that nosy Ellen, and I had just enough time to avoid her. I hurriedly took my cup of coffee and as I walked towards my office I heard her voice calling me, but I pretended not to, I just gave her a simple nod, I was in a hurry. I hoped she wouldn't follow me, and fortunately, she didn't. That woman was very good at minding other people's business and didn't know when to stop. Once locked in my fortress, in my hands the steaming cup of coffee, I thought of John and Mary. Unfortunately, since the day of their children's funeral, I still hadn't been able to get to the hospital for a visit, so I didn't even know how they were doing. I couldn't let any more days go by, no...I couldn't do that. John had paid the ultimate price, and I was sure he would want a friendly shoulder to cry on and vent to. Good thing I had gotten the address of the hospital from a mutual friend of ours.

The nurse at the front desk was doing some paperwork and didn't notice my arrival. I politely asked her about the room where Mrs. Brown was staying, but she politely pointed out that visiting hours would start in ten minutes, so she pointed me to the waiting room and assured me that she would let me know immediately when it was time to go in. I thanked her and headed into the waiting room. It was a room with old prints on the walls (I noticed that the Christmas decorations were already starting to appear), a few tables with some old and outdated magazines, and the classic waiting chairs. I took a seat next to the snack and soft drink vending machine, just in case I felt like something to drink. I put the box of milk chocolates with hazelnuts in the chair next to mine, crossed my hands behind my neck and little by little I stretched my legs more and more in a not very elegant but relaxing position for me. The cold day with some clouds scattered in the sky made me appreciate the warmth emanating from the heating system of the room. A warmth that could conciliate the sleep even on those uncomfortable chairs, rigid and cold as marble. I closed my eyes for a brief moment and let myself be lulled: « You too in this valley of pain?».

I opened my eyes and saw him sitting in front of me. I could hardly recognize him, he had changed so much since the last time I had seen him. His eyes were hollow, his beard was unkempt for several days, and he was so thin that his suit was almost three sizes too big. John could now be considered the ghost of himself. Only a shadow remained of his former air.

« John... How are you?» I asked, getting up from the chair and going towards him.

Redemption days

‹‹ I won't lie to you, also because I can't do it, and then you know how I am, I understood it from your look before››.

‹‹ I'm sorry... I didn't mean to...››

‹‹ No problem. I could very well be in a movie about zombies and I wouldn't need makeup›› and laugh.

A bitter, sultry laugh.

‹‹ You came to see Mary, didn't you?››

‹‹ Yes... maybe I should have told you earlier, I'm sorry››.

‹‹ Don't say that, even in jest. Mary will be pleased to have a visit from an old and dear friend. Come on, let's go to her››.

‹‹ It's not visiting hours yet,›› I told him as I checked the time on my wristwatch. Five minutes had not yet passed since I entered the building.

‹‹ Who told you it wasn't visiting hours?››

‹‹ The nurse in the lobby. I sat here waiting››

‹‹ Don't worry, just follow me››.

I gathered my coat from the chair and the small present for the resident and stood behind him. Furthermore, I only noticed at that instant that John was walking with the aid of a cane, perhaps the bullet had done more damage than was suspected. We passed in front of the counter and with a calm manner, John greeted the nurse who returned with a gentle smile.

‹‹ See? Now and then a smile opens a door››.

Room 197.

Single room.

The door was closed and before knocking to enter, my friend made some important recommendations for meeting his wife. He had to do this every time, no mistake could be made that could somehow deal Mary the death blow. Orders from the doctor who had been treating her. Unfortunately, the woman had erased the painful memories of that cursed day, a sort of self-defense, while the memories before the event were clouded and confused. They made her believe that Arthur was at his mother's house, and to calm her down, they decided to have a boy with a voice like Arthur's call her from time to time.

Redemption days

A macabre game, as he called it, but useful to justify Arthur's absence and as far as he was concerned, he had injured his leg while fixing the gutters, falling from the ladder a few weeks ago. The room had few but essential furnishings, definitely depressing. The walls were an indefinite color, sort of cross between light blue and pale purple, and the only colorful note I noticed inside the room was the flowers in the center of the small table. A few books peeped out on the nightstand next to the bed: I didn't pay much attention to the titles, but I remembered that Mary was a book devourer. The room also had a private bathroom without a window, which was one more way to increase the patient's privacy. That accommodation, while not high-end, had to cost a lot of money, and how much could John make it for? The health insurance covered only a part and for a short period, then all the expenses would have to be paid by them and at that point, they would have to decide whether to continue the care or not. And he would choose the latter. Mary sat on the edge of the bed wearing an embroidered pink robe. A simple, well-groomed hairstyle, her face lightly made up to give her a pleasant appearance, even in front of her few visitors. As soon as she saw her husband appear, she lit up with joy, stood up to meet him, and embrace him, pressing an affectionate kiss on his lips, as if they had been sweethearts. John returned those gestures of love, but he made sure to take her back to bed and make her lie down or at most sit up.

‹‹ Darling, you know you need to rest. The doctor doesn't want you to make unnecessary efforts, given your precarious condition. Come on, sit on the edge of the bed››.

‹‹ The doctors! What do they know about how I feel... I could climb a mountain in front of them! Darling, you worry too much››.

‹‹ Don't overdo it now, climb a mountain. You haven't fully recovered yet, so you have to follow the directives of the doctor who knows what he's doing... and then you have visitors today››.

I had remained behind my friend, out of his field of vision, waiting for the green light.

‹‹ Arthur? Arthur has finally returned and decided to visit me, hasn't he? Come on in, son...››.

Her eyes lit up with joy at being able to see the boy again but, unfortunately for her, her husband had to cut short those hopes and I knew it wasn't the first time, and perhaps it wouldn't be the last. He reassured her and held her in a consoling hug, then with a small hand gesture, he made me sit inside the room.

‹‹ How are you, Mary? You look great!›› I said, handing her the small present I had brought her. John intercepted the box between our two hands and took it to put it in the drawer of the bedside table.

She thanked me with a slight smile and justified her husband's gesture by explaining that the doctors had prevented her from eating sweets. The conversation focused on Arthur, although John tried to divert her to other topics, she was stubborn. She could hardly hold back her tears. In the end, we said goodbye with the solemn promise that we would all meet again at their house for dinner.

Redemption days

She, John, Arthur (she didn't even remember that she was pregnant and had lost the baby, poor woman), Lorelain, and I would go back to the life we had always lived, close to our loved ones.

As we were heading out the door to grab a bite to eat at a diner a few steps from the hospital (John had been eating there since the first day of his wife's hospitalization) my friend remembered that he needed to talk to Mary's doctor, so he asked me to do him a favor and promised me that he would do it quickly and buy me a nice lunch. I didn't let him tell me again, as I was in no hurry. I followed him in silence through the departments to the elevator that would take us to the fifth floor of the building. The elevator doors opened and in front of us and to my surprise I saw a sign on which were printed some rules of conduct to be kept in that department. My friend approached the nurse, chatted with her for a few minutes, and then led the way along a cold and immaculate corridor lined on one side with windows, and on the other with rooms with glass windows obscured by curtains. There was something sinister about the intensive care unit. He stopped in front of room number 5, one of the few without a curtain, and I saw him. Surrounded by all sorts of ultra-modern equipment with several small tubes coming out of his body to end up inside those metal boxes that had the task of keeping him alive was James. We were separated only by a glass window. John remained silent. I remained silent and observed him. I watched that motionless body. I was looking at James! Our victim! My victim! Arthur's fiance... his son! The pest... the unclean being!

‹‹ How long have you known about this?›› I asked him, as he was beginning to enjoy the baked potatoes he had ordered as a side dish to the beefsteak.

‹‹ Three days after Mary's hospitalization and by a simple coincidence››

‹‹ Why did you bring me to him?››

John put down his fork, and to my surprise placed his hand on top of mine. He squeezed it lightly.

His empty, melancholic eyes lingered on mine and then resumed the conversation: ‹‹ To understand! I did it for this reason!››

‹‹ To understand? What should I understand?››

‹‹ The horror we committed››

‹‹ He deserved it... he deserved it...›› I repeated without conviction.

‹‹ You know it's not true! That gesture changed us... our hands are stained with innocent blood!››.

I freed myself from that grip and instinctively looked at my hands, and in that instant, it seemed to me that they oozed blood. James' blood! Arthur's blood! The little girl's blood! I snapped to my feet and ran to the bathroom to wash my hands. I scrubbed them vigorously using an exaggerated amount of liquid soap, but the damned blood wouldn't go away, and then the water coming out of the faucet turned a dark red color too... I was washing with blood! The scream nipped in the bud as tears streaked down my face.

Redemption days

‹‹ You needed that vision to make you fully understand the evil we have committed! We are monsters!››.

I turned towards him and with tears in my eyes, I embraced him in a liberating and protective embrace. Finally, I had found inner peace.

‹‹ Courage, old man! We finish lunch. If someone comes in and sees us hugging, they might think we're a couple, and you're not my type! Come on››.

A line that normally would have never been uttered by either of us. We returned to our table a little more serene.

‹‹ Now let's eat and then resume the discussion››.
‹‹ Don't worry, we can talk about it right now... I don't think I'll be able to eat anything else, my stomach is in knots››.

I pushed the plate away with an irritated gesture as if it gave off a nauseating smell.

‹‹ John, I'm confused... I've been watching the sunrise for months. When I try to close my eyes, I see those damn scenes again... from James to Thanksgiving night, to my divorce and the argument with Lorelain during the funeral... I'm going crazy!››.
‹‹ Welcome to the club!››.

A club I could have happily done without being a member of. What I couldn't understand was why it was only now that all the remorse was coming to the surface, after all, I hadn't always had a clear conscience. In some of our acts, there were also several deaths, but the feelings I had were of joy and never of remorse. Why then had everything changed?

‹‹ What has happened to us?›› I asked with a slight tremor in my voice. John finished his lunch and then said: ‹‹ We're murderers only when we act as a group and on behalf of the association! But taken individually, no. Unity is strength!››. Occasionally he would stop to look out the window at the many people passing by on their way to who knows where.

‹‹ When I heard about Arthur's homosexuality, I was so angry I couldn't see straight, and I was afraid of what others might think... the gossip... the jokes... the comments made in whispers. My mind was foggy to the point that I just wanted to avenge the shame. Unfortunately, I didn't stop to talk to my son, to try to understand his world and comprehend his state of mind, but instead, I went in the opposite direction and popped straight into hell. I turned into a monster that night. You saw how I lashed out at that boy, the fury, and joy I felt with every blow I struck, feeling him give in little by little... My God! A soulless monster! I have no excuse!››.

My friend was about to collapse under the weight of guilt for that tragedy. He ran his fingers over his eyes to wipe away the first tears.

‹‹ John stop torturing yourself! You haven't fully recovered, and you can't afford to go crazy or Mary will be alone!››

Redemption days

‹‹ No. We have to free ourselves, we can't keep running away for fear of losing our minds.››

‹‹ Listen to me.››

‹‹ Listen, it's not a problem for me. I can live with it, but not you.›› I lied, knowing I was lying.

‹‹ Damn it! Why the fuck do you keep pretending? I want to remind you of your reaction after you saw James. Your tears and your desperation for that boy clearly show that you are going through your ordeal, but you keep pretending that you are not. You adored James, you had taken a liking to him from the beginning and little by little you were considering him as family. Don't tell me no, because I wouldn't believe it and neither would you››.

No, I could no longer deny it.

‹‹ Don't worry, the journey has just begun, and I can tell you that it won't be pleasant, but day by day the ghosts will disappear... trust what I tell you, I've been going through it since Thanksgiving. You don't have to rush it. The situation within the association?›› he asked with a touch of curiosity.

‹‹ Big changes at the top››.

Big and nebulous.

‹‹ Don't tell me that 'Rat Face' won the first prize? Don't tell me... fuck!››

‹‹ He had to settle for the consolation prize. The first prize in the lottery went to someone else››.

‹‹ Strange... I thought he was the winner. Who's the new asshole in the control room anyway?››

‹‹ Pleased to meet you... I'm the asshole››.

At that sentence he was interdicted, then he apologized: ‹‹ I didn't remember that you were running too... I'm sorry!››

‹‹ No problem. You weren't yourself after all. And maybe I should have given up on the race... I shouldn't have participated››

‹‹ We were both victims of him.››

‹‹ You mean the old boss?››

‹‹ For him, we are only pawns that he moves as he wants on his mental chessboard››.

Pawns and nothing more.

‹‹ Bastard gave me the weapon to ruin my family. Don't ask me why... because I don't know, but I'm sure he's behind your election››.

John knew a few details that I was missing that might have helped us carry out our plan. But I had to figure out if he was still on our side, or if he wanted to stay on the sidelines. And if he stayed there, I would know.

Redemption days

‹‹ You see, you were elected instead of Rat Face, a man who would do anything to please the old boss, and who would never think for himself... so if he wanted to continue running the organization from behind the lines, he was the man to do it with, not you››.

‹‹ I see you've come to the same conclusion as we have, too.››

‹‹ Who else is involved?››

‹‹ Phil and Matt and you may have some more information. If you want to tell, go ahead. Greatest discretion though.››

John assumed a serious and sad expression at the same time. He wanted to talk, to let off steam, but he knew very well that with those revelations he would have lit the fuse for an internal conflict in the association with unexpected results. He did not back down. Behind the discovery of Arthur's homosexuality, there was the hand of the old boss, as well as the tip of the exact day of the attack on that club. The idea of the stakeout and the punitive expedition, fixed in that precise place, day, and time, was not all Oscar Bell's doing. So, John discovered that it was the old man himself who organized the whole thing, with the solemn promise that no one inside would know who the real creator was. Not to mention the fact that Deep Throat, a.k.a. the grand old man, had taken the trouble to inform his squire, a.k.a. Rat Face. At that point, the old man knew very well that James was my subordinate and at the same time Arthur's fiance. Little by little the pieces were fitting together, but we were still a long way from figuring out the complete picture. To get there, we would have to answer one question: 'What is the ultimate goal?' John was on our side and would certainly give us his moral support, and that was it. He decided to stay out of it.

‹‹ The secret archive?››

‹‹ It exists and the only person who has access to all that information is him!››

‹‹ Always him. But why was he so sure of the existence of the archive?››

‹‹ Have you seen it?››

‹‹ Listen carefully, what I'm about to tell you must remain secret. I haven't told you anything. Swear to me on the graves of my children!››

‹‹ I swear. You know you can trust me. I would never betray you!››

‹‹ A few days after my two sons' funerals, I dared to set foot in that house again and start living, as much as I could. Two days after my return, I received an unexpected visit and I confess that when I opened the door and saw him there on my doorstep, I got shivers down my spine. He appeared to give me the final blow, knowing well of the investigations I had made among a small circle of trusted associates. Once inside the house, he focused his gaze on the exact spot where... you know››.

I knew very well what he was referring to.

Redemption days

‹‹ At that very moment, I had the feeling of catching a glimpse of evil in his eyes, mixed with joy and satisfaction. Let's face it, I may have been wrong about that, but I digress. Excuse me. You know as well as I do that that being doesn't use turns of phrase and when he wants to strike, he strikes straight on without hiding. He did it that time too. He was ordering me to leave the association without raising any fuss either inside or outside, and do you know why? Simply because I had completed my task. At that point I took him head-on and let out all the anger I had in my body, telling him everything I thought about him and Arthur's story, and in that surge of anger, swore that I would not leave the association without fighting him and that I would stop only when I saw him defeated. He didn't move a muscle. No expression.

He pulled a black file out of his jacket and threw it on the table››

‹‹ Excuse me, the interruption... was it from that phantom archive?››

He nodded his head in the affirmative, then resumed the story: ‹‹ In that dossier, my whole life was written in detail, both inside and outside the association. Reading it, I found many episodes, even years old. Some of them even dated back to my university period. I also saw some photos taken without my knowledge... I can tell you that one portrayed me at the funeral››.

He quivered with rage.

‹‹ That archive exists, and you can be sure that each one of you has your personnel file, ready to be used.››

John made me understand that the spying didn't stop at the archive but also included recordings of phone calls, and reading of e-mails and that also the cell phones were kept under control. That bastard had built up over the years a thick network of spying worthy of the CIA and used it for his damned business. We said goodbye.

From that moment I went every day to that damned gray and gloomy building, located on the other side of the city. I climbed the steps slowly, but one day I got stuck in front of the door. I couldn't find the keys.

Those damn things were playing tricks on me and I had the doubt that I had forgotten them in the house or the office, I tried to think back and mentally review all the moves of the day. Damn it! I had forgotten them inside the car... what a pain in the ass! I walked back to the car, slightly annoyed at the setback. I didn't feel like going back and forth... I was even tempted to get in the car and go home to relax. Instead, a note folded under the windshield made me give up that idea.

Written and printed by a PC. A few words and no signature.

"Friend you have started a war that you will not be able to finish. Give up, there is still time to do so."

Redemption days

A friend or a warning? We missed that too, so the old man already knew everything and... fuck. I tore the damn note into a thousand pieces, then started the car and headed home. Fuck him! At the last moment, I changed my mind for the umpteenth time about what to do. I would have warned the others later, I didn't feel the need to alarm them unnecessarily.

At home, I had a nice hot shower, a per-cooked meal, and a few cans of beer to help me sleep.

The first to know about the note was John. I met him at the hospital because from the day he showed me, James, I continued to go to the hospital once a week. First I would visit Mary, and then in John's company (other times alone), I would visit him. It was on one of those occasions that I talked to my friend about the note. He, too, felt that it could only say one thing: 'The old man knew everything! And he was preparing for battle'.

‹‹ We need to call a meeting out of town for this weekend. Gather all the people you deem trustworthy and talk about the situation... however... first alert them to the text of the note and stand by››
‹‹ Wait for what?››
‹‹ That one of them doesn't say they have the same note, right?››
‹‹ Do you think there is a spy among us?››
‹‹ Yes, he'll be the one who won't talk about his card. Did you think you were so important that you were the only one who got the notice?››.

I wasn't that significant. I asked him if he had also received it and his answer was affirmative. He showed it to me and I noticed that the text was the same as mine. Maybe the bastard had made them in series. John was not going to follow us. There I summoned one by one. They all agreed to attend the meeting, but none of them mentioned a possible anonymous note. I didn't worry too much, I would investigate in person during the meeting.

I gave each of the directions to the designated location, a nature park a few kilometers outside the city. A secluded place with a picnic area with tables and benches, where they could sit away from prying eyes and discuss the situation to take the necessary countermeasures. Each of us would go to the location indicated, but I recommended that they take different routes on the way there and back, and to keep their eyes open.

I parked in the main parking lot, walked the few meters that separated me from the meeting point, and realized I was the first. I looked at the time and realized that I had arrived a good half hour early, so I could only wait for them to sit on a bench. Fortunately from that position, there was a good view of the parking lot and, for better or worse, I remembered almost all the cars of my friends, so I put myself on the lookout. An hour passed before the first of the summonses showed up: Nicolas Smith.

Redemption days

During the electoral campaign, he spontaneously approached our current with much enthusiasm and a desire to work to ease my election. Smith could be considered the classic man of the apparatus and loyal to the cause, and perhaps he wasn't very subtle during certain actions. Almost two meters tall, black eyes, thick reddish hair with freckles that covered almost his entire face, a detail of which he was perhaps ashamed. Married with three children, fervent republican to the extreme, and a well-paid steady job, let's say that he was not doing badly. Seeing him coming from the parking lot with his classic cowboy gait, I remembered that he was the first to congratulate himself on the success of the punitive expedition and that he regretted not having participated, pointing out that if he had been there, the bastard would have tasted his iron club all over his body and would never have gotten up again. Chills ran down my spine at those memories.

‹‹ Hello Nicolas, welcome. As you can see, you're the first,›› I said, going up to him to shake his hand.

‹‹ I see, but where are all the others? Don't tell me I'm the only one?››

‹‹ For the moment, yes, and at this point, I think you're the only one who has accepted the invitation››.

‹‹ My dear, you have surrounded yourself with only cowards but don't worry because I will stand by you in the fight. You can trust me!›› clenched his fist at the level of his heart as a sign of loyalty.

We talked about the elections, and he asked me for more details about the tactics to be followed for the good of the association, and he didn't spare some jabs at the old leader, but he didn't say anything about a possible note. This detail kept me from delving into some aspects of the action plan and from talking about the note I had received. In the end, we headed for our respective cars to return to our homes. We said our goodbyes and I made arrangements for our next meeting after the Christmas holidays, which were almost upon us.

Smith merely nodded in the affirmative. I watched him pull out of the parking lot and take the main road back into town, while I sat by my car thinking about the meeting.

When I got home, I found another surprise. An envelope, devoid of sender and addressee, well-sealed and deposited by hand inside my letterbox. I knew very well what it contained.

Dear friend, your army has vanished, and you are left with only one soldier. Give it up, there's still time. A trusted friend'.

The friend knew about the meeting and its progress. I reduced the whole thing into a thousand pieces and threw them in the bin. The next day I made a round of calls to find out the reasons for the absences. Each of them had received the note, but it also contained a threat of retaliation if they didn't leave me alone.

Redemption days

At first, they all hesitated before speaking, but then gradually they spilled the beans. I didn't blame them for their behavior, after all, they had a family to protect, and once that round of phone calls was over, I realized I was left alone with that damned spy Nicolas Smith!

The only one who hadn't said anything to me about a possible threatening note. Fuck! I had fallen into the net like a simple rookie! Fuck! They had made scorched earth around me, perhaps in the hope that I too would desist from my action and fall in line to become his docile lapdog in service of the old man. But he still hadn't understood who he was dealing with, that filthy bastard! I wasn't going to give up, and I was going to get to the bottom of this, even if it meant prison or, worse, death. The next move would be made after the holidays now I had more important and private business to attend to.

Christmas had passed quietly. I hadn't celebrated it. There was a time when the house would have been lit up by the lights on the tree and small decorations, scattered a bit throughout the house, but not that year. No gifts to buy and no surprises for the gift my Lorelain received. Nothing. I was left alone and sad. Holed up in the house, locked between grief and anger at the turn my life had taken. I also took some vacation time off, which allowed me to return to work in mid-January.

Three days after I finalized my divorce with Lorelain, I obtained a loan from my bank to pay my ex-wife for her share of the house, which then became mine. She didn't push me too hard during the final divorce negotiations. Each month I had to pay her a child support check of about $2,000 until she found a new husband. In my heart, I hoped to continue paying alimony, since deep down I still wanted her.

During the holidays I had tried to contact John to wish him a happy birthday and, at the same time, to ask about his wife's health, but both the home phone and the cell phone remained silent. I didn't even go to the hospital to visit James or Mary: I felt guilty about those failures, but I didn't want to see anyone. Yet, noticing that John wasn't returning my calls, I decided to stop by the clinic and found out that my friend had signed his wife out four days before Christmas.

The nurse who gave me the information, left me almost immediately to return to her duties, but before leaving she politely told me that if I wanted more information I could ask for Dr. Hincks, who would be taking over the same department in about an hour. I thanked her and left her to her duties. While waiting to meet Dr. Hincks (hoping that he would receive me) I took the elevator and in a few seconds I was in the 'Intensive Care Unit'. James. It's been a long time... maybe a little too long... Even though I didn't externalize it, I thought about it all the time... James.

I walked confidently towards the room he was in and once I got there I noticed it was empty. I checked the number above the door. 4. Was that it... then?

Redemption days

‹‹ Pardon me, the boy who was in room number 4? Mr. James Hoffman?›› the nurse said affably.

At that answer, I widened my eyes. I realized I didn't even know his last name! I nodded shyly in the affirmative, trying to hide my shame at my lack of knowledge.

‹‹ He is no longer in this ward. His condition has improved, so he has been transferred to another ward, on the third floor.››

‹‹ Thank you, may I know your new room number?››

‹‹ You should inquire at the reception desk on the floor, surely my colleague will be able to help you››

‹‹ Thank you for your availability. Have a nice day››

‹‹ Don't mention it. Have a nice day.››

I still had some time before I went to see Dr. Hincks about John's matter, so I could have visited James, but how would he take it? Maybe the nurses on the ward had told him about my visits and John's... Did he know that, on that dramatic night, I was there or not? Perhaps he suspected it... maybe he knew everything... No! I decided to give up going to him. Unfortunately, a doubt peeped into my already tormented mind: if he had finally regained consciousness, had the authorities already been in touch with him for any answers about that cursed night? What if he had spoken? Impossible... if he had talked, I would have been behind bars by now on charges of attempted homophobic murder. He didn't recognize me. I could be sure of that.

Dr. Hincks welcomed me into his office. Small, sterile, and with essential furniture, four reproductions of 'famous' paintings on the desk, some folders, and two frames that portrayed him in the company of his family. He made me sit down and without many pleasantries informed me of the patient's situation, warning me that the conversation was strictly confidential.

‹‹ In this last period I have seen her several times to visit the patient and I have also noticed their close relationship with her husband, for this reason, I want to have a conversation with her, also because I know she was among those present at that tragedy. She didn't know about the resignation either, did she? So I believe that no one was notified››.

‹‹ Nobody? That's not like him››.

‹‹ I thought so, but that's not the only inconsistency in the story, unfortunately.››

‹‹ What do you mean?›› I asked.

‹‹ Listen to me, it is not my nature to interfere in the private life of my patients, but this time is different. I had been treating the lady since the first day of admission and, frankly, the time had not yet come to stop the therapies, but unfortunately, the husband did not want to hear any reason and signed taking responsibility for the early discharge. The last time I saw him, I made him promise me that he would call me at any time of the day or night, in case any problem arose... instead...››

‹‹ I know him very well, and I am sure that they are at home, and that everything is going well...››.

Redemption days

‹‹ Unfortunately it is not. We have called their home a couple of times since the resignation and have not heard back. This fact worries me a lot. The lady is in no condition to bear the harsh reality in one go››

‹‹ Next of kin?››.

I'm sure they had contacted the relatives before me, but... ‹‹ Look, they assured us that they would be in touch as soon as they had any information, but until today we have not received any communication. We believe that they have been instructed not to let anything out of the family circle. A sort of protective cordon››.

‹‹ What should I do?››

‹‹ Being a friend of yours, you could go to their house for a simple visit and get some useful information about the actual status of the patient and report to me what you think is abnormal. We don't use this kind of practice, but this case is special››.

I accepted and before leaving he gave me his business card with all the phone numbers.

Another problem to solve is if I didn't have more urgent and dangerous ones to deal with, but for John, I would have given my own life and also perhaps because I felt partly responsible for that situation. He didn't answer the phone. I tried several times, but it always rang off the hook. I stopped by that afternoon. The garden was uncultivated. The windows were barred and closed to the point that not even a thread of light filtered through. The mail piled up, the newspapers from many days old piled up in disorder on the doorstep, all this didn't tell me anything good. No sign of recent life. I rang the doorbell. No answer. I knocked on the door with my fists hard and firm. Nothing. I called out to them, so they could hear me from inside. Still no answer. The house seemed to have been unoccupied for a fortnight, since the day Mary had been discharged from the hospital, so she hadn't taken her home but somewhere else... but where? And for what reason? A tangled situation... damn it! I didn't know which way to turn and finally decided to try to get in. I went through the back of the house and watched for a few more minutes before going inside, hoping that some neighbor wouldn't call 911 to report an attempted theft. The playground was in the same state as it was that damn day, it almost seemed as if time had stood still. I knocked on the back door, and as in previous attempts there was no answer, but in this case, I noticed a detail that made me hope for some presence inside the house: the kitchen light was on! I could glimpse it from behind the window curtain, but I didn't see anyone, and this made me have further doubts. I picked up a rusty iron bar from the ground and with a sharp blow I broke the glass of the secondary door, just enough to get my hand through and open it with confidence. The noise was dry, and some pieces fell inside. I carefully removed the remaining pieces with the bar (all I needed was to cut my wrist!), then... CLICK!

Redemption days

I entered the house.

An intense smell of closed penetrated my nostrils with violence. I had to hold back a gag reflex. I left the door slightly ajar in a vain attempt to change the air, although I thought it was useless. Everything was in order. Not a pin out of place. I checked the fridge and to my surprise, I noticed that it was empty. I went to the other rooms and found the same situation. The idea that John had taken his wife to another place was taking shape, maybe first he had devoted himself to cleaning the house, and meanwhile, I had broken into private property and would be arrested.

‹‹ John! It's me… John… Mary, are you home?› I shouted.

I wanted to make sure that no one was there, the theories that were in my mind had not convinced me completely. I had to be sure that John had taken his wife to a quieter place free of sad memories. Without realizing it, I found myself in the living room. The place where the tragedy had occurred. The memories of that day came back to my mind as if they were a projection of an old horror movie. I rushed into the adjoining room to try to calm down. I wanted to scream with rage and pain. At that point, I decided to go upstairs to finish the check and make my peace with it. The stairs creaked with every step, John had never decided to fix them, he always put off that maintenance, and Mary complained and sang at him.

I smiled at those memories, and when I reached the top floor, I turned on the hallway light and saw that the doors to the rooms were all closed. I went to Arthur's and opened the door, just to stick my head in and take a quick look. I found it in perfect order. If I remembered correctly, John had fixed it up for his son's return, and perhaps it had remained like that since the day of the tragedy. The bed had been made, there was a brand-new laptop on the desk (the old PC had been destroyed in a fit of rage), and on the shelves, some comic books had been carefully arranged. I closed the door and went to the master bedroom. I turned the handle and opened the door.

I found the light switch, pressed it, and then I saw John and Mary. I had found them. He was sitting in an old rocking chair with a wool blanket covering his legs, his face turned in the direction of the closed window, while Mary was lying in bed, dressed as if for a fancy dinner. I approached my friend and touched his arm: he was as cold as marble! The police arrived a few minutes after my 911 call. The coroner and two hearses also arrived. The officers searched the entire house from top to bottom, especially the room where the murder-suicide had taken place.

During my interrogation, I explained to the officer on duty the reason for my trespassing and thought that perhaps they were holding me responsible for their deaths; fortunately, Dr. Hincks confirmed my version, but I had to remain on hand. The garden in front of the house was already filled with curious onlookers kept at a distance by the classic yellow cordon, it was repeating the same scenery of Thanksgiving.

Redemption days

Once I got home, I had another surprise. A messenger delivered a letter. No sender or anything else could be traced back to the mysterious figure. It was a normal, white envelope with my address typed on it, perhaps it was a ploy to prevent me from recognizing the handwriting, I immediately thought of another notice from the old man but when I opened it, I was stunned. The letter had been written to me from beyond, from John. In those lines, my friend justified his extreme gesture.

"My dear friend, by the time you read this letter, Mary and I will be gone. I didn't know whether to write you or not, but in the end, I decided that you should know the reasons for our actions. We have always been very close, and I wanted to leave this world peacefully. Unfortunately, I couldn't continue to keep Mary in the hospital, the insurance would have covered another five days of treatment in the clinic, and the costs I would have had to incur were huge. Not to mention that my world no longer existed. Day after day my visits became more and more unbearable, not to mention Mary's constant requests to meet Arthur... and I cowardly made up an excuse every time and hated myself for it. Every night I spent thinking about how to get out of this tragic situation, and finally, I found the solution. The first step was to get Mary released from the hospital and then lock us in the house for some time. You see, I wanted to spend the last few days in her company. I told her that Arthur would be home shortly – my final lie. I didn't want her to suffer, so I decided to give her a strong dose of sleeping pills, and before she fell asleep forever, I gave her a last kiss and asked God's forgiveness for that act. Not only that, but I spent a whole night waking up, sitting in the rocking chair, and then I too took my dose of sleeping pill. I ask you to forgive me and I would like you to do me one last favor: we both would like to be buried next to our children, at least we will be united in death. Farewell forever, my dear friend. Forgive me for the pain I caused you with my choice, but I had no more strength to go on. Your John, Mary, Arthur, and little Janet."

Tears were streaming down my face. I couldn't believe that he had done that, even though I was the one who found the bodies and, ironically, that was the very night I received that letter. I felt a sense of impotence and anger. Likewise, I decided to keep it and pretend nothing had happened.

Redemption days

I reluctantly decided not to show up at the funeral, so I watched the ceremony from a secluded corner of the cemetery, away from prying eyes. Few people had shown up, no one from the association, and I didn't even see the missing members of our group. None. A few days later I read in the local chronicle a paragraph about the disaster, I read the first lines, but I stopped. I did not want to continue to read that nonsense and went to the page of obituaries and read the one of the association in which it said to cry for the tragic untimely death of the brotherly friend and wife. Hypocrites and bastards to the end! They had forgotten to write that they had given the fatal blow to John! The old man had had his victory over us. John could no longer bother them and as for me, I was now in complete isolation within the association. Everyone carefully avoided me, and worse still, even those that I considered the most trustworthy and safe cut me off. I had to choose whether to become a 'Pinocchio' manipulated by 'Mangiafuoco', leave the association, or wait to end up like John.

I went to the cemetery to visit John. Likewise, I placed the bouquets at each grave, one for each of them, and stood there thinking. Four headstones. Side by side. Cold marble. Dates are carved simply. Serene photos. Smiles of a time that could never return. The grave of a life never born. The only one without photos. The tombstone that clutched the heart. I felt my eyes moist. I was crying. Furthermore, I stood in front of my friend's final resting place for a long time, staring at those faces, and with my mind, I went searching for memories of the days we spent together with our respective families. But at once the images of that cursed night of unprecedented violence and blood-red Thanksgiving made their way back to me. The epilogue of that event was still fresh... maybe I could have saved them... if I had realized how John was, I could have avoided the last massacre... instead... nothing!

‹‹ Did you come to see the outcome of your betrayal?››.

I turned sharply and saw him standing before me. His arm was bandaged, tied around his neck, dark glasses to hide the swellings, and a cane to support himself and walk. The young man wasn't being subtle, and he had a point, he knew all about it.

‹‹ You're out of the hospital and I see you're recovering. I'm happy for you.››
‹‹ I may be recovering physically... but the memories will last a lifetime!››
‹‹ Listen to me, James...››
‹‹ You listen to me! You owe it to him too!››
‹‹ I'm sorry. I...››

Redemption days

‹‹ When I regained consciousness after my time in intensive care, two officers came to question me about the attack, my mind put up a wall of self-defense to hide the face of the Judas and the tormentor! The only person to whom I had opened my heart to confide and ask for help had turned out to be a Judas, while the torturer was none other than Arthur's father. My partner! I didn't spill the beans for one simple reason. A nurse told me about the visits I had received during my stay in the hospital, and two, in particular, caught my attention: yours and John's. John came to see me every day. Above all, John came to see me every day, always asked about my state of health, and sometimes brought me a few changes of clothing while you stopped to read me a few pages of a book, even though you knew I couldn't hear it. Your repentance was genuine, it certainly wouldn't give me Arthur back, but at least I knew that remorse wouldn't be with you all your life. All your life...››.

His speech left me speechless, I didn't know what to say or do.

‹‹ This doesn't mean I have forgiven you, but...››
‹‹ James listen...››
‹‹ Goodbye!››.

I stood there alone. I would never get his forgiveness, and maybe I would never forgive myself for the evil I had committed. My hands were dripping with innocent blood, and not even a hundred lives would be enough to redeem me from my evil. Once I was in the car, I turned my cell phone back on and got a call back from the old bastard. I decided to call him back at once to get rid of that task. I hated his smart-ass tone more and more! The call was brief, the famous preparatory meeting for our clamorous gesture could not be postponed any longer, and since I was the new boss, it was up to me to call it; but the old man only wanted me to give my approval to the date he had before decided on, which I did without much trouble. I had to give him the impression that I had become his puppet, and in the meantime, I would continue with my plan.

I arrived at the office an hour before the official start of the meeting. Likewise, I entered through the main entrance, greeting the few members I passed on my way to 'my' office, where I would barricade myself until the meeting started. I needed to gather my thoughts and come up with one to postpone the attack. As soon as I entered, I had the unpleasant surprise of finding the bastard sitting in the armchair, his ever-present stinking cigar between his lips, intent on impregnating the whole room with that stench.

‹‹ I didn't expect to see you at this hour. The meeting is still a long way away,›› he said, letting a cloud of smoke escape from those small and insignificant lips.
‹‹ I could say the same.››
‹‹ Shot and sunk! ›› and laughed heartily.

Redemption days

Damn him! With kindness, I pointed out where he was sitting, but he pretended not to understand and remained in his place. A clear signal that it was still him to dictate law within the association, and that the undersigned had to submit to his power. In the end, I decided to leave the room and go in search of a place where I could calmly cool off. Also, because if I had stayed in there, I could have jumped on him and throttled him with my own hands... and maybe it would have been the final solution to my problems and sorrows, but I would have gone back to what I was before, and I didn't want to do that. The inner change had begun, and the process was irreversible. Unfortunately, I hadn't been able to find that damned secret archive, nor had I been able to talk to the outsiders: in essence, I was still stuck at the starting blocks. In the end, my wandering through the rooms of the association led me to the stairs to the basement, and I don't know why I went down them and entered. From the dust and dirt that was there, I thought I was the first living thing to enter that area in several years. The light bulb was acting up and flickering. A nuisance to the eyes.

The smell of dampness mixed with the smell of mold made me slightly dizzy but it only took a few minutes to get used to it... and damn! Without realizing it, I bumped into a stack of boxes, dropping them on the floor and raising a fuss that made me cough. I had to be more careful how I moved down there, even if no one was going down there, I had to leave a few traces of my passage... So I bent down and began to pick up and arrange the boxes and their contents as best I could. I found everything! A small dump, that's what that basement was! Antique radios, old beer cans, some gas cans, and other items that were no longer needed. While I was putting them back in place, my attention was caught by an object. Next to the fallen pile, I noticed a metal box, army style. I decided to use it as a base to place the boxes, but after placing three of them, curiosity got the better of me, so with a well-aimed blow I dropped the cardboard tower back to the ground and bent down to get a better look at it.

Metal. Cold. Hard. Discolored. Padlocked.

Redemption days

No clue to the owner, just an embossed alphanumeric series above the lid: 754/ABG. I tried to figure out its contents by lifting it off the ground. It didn't weigh much, but I gave a few shakes to hear the sound of the contents... almost non-existent. I put it back on the floor, and with my eyes, I looked around for some useful tool to break the lock and pry inside. No luck. Unfortunately, I had to go back up to the surface for the meeting, but I decided to get a hammer to open it later. It may or may not have contained interesting old documents (it certainly wasn't the archive), at best I would have taken it home to use again, and no one would have noticed it was missing. I quickly cleaned up my clothes and walked out of the basement, taking care not to be noticed by any of my brothers. Finally, I headed into the main hall.

Opening the door, I found all the members seated in their respective seats, while the old man was comfortably settled in his rightful place. The buzz ceased immediately as I entered the room. I greeted them all with the best 'fake' smile I had available in my countless collection of 'bronze faces' and made my way to the only remaining free chair on the side of the table. Facing each other. Ready for the fight. Him with his army, me alone. None of my so-called 'friends' or 'soldiers' had shown up, it felt like I was in front of a courtroom, not a meeting, and I was the defendant! Next to the old man, I noticed his lackey all smiling and amused by the situation with a smile on his cocked face, telling me: 'I won the war!' He had indeed won, but not the war! All eyes were on me and some looks didn't bode well, but I held on. I couldn't afford to give in to their accusing looks.

‹‹ We welcome our new president. Early as always, and since we're all finally here, we can start the meeting... if of course the boss agrees.››

‹‹ No problem. And I give you the floor again to introduce the main topic››

‹‹ I don't want to go over your head. I'm retired now, and you should consider me just an ordinary member of our community, without any leadership position››

‹‹ I insist!››

‹‹ It must be the president who introduces each meeting, our bylaws provide for this and until now this has always been the practice››

‹‹ I know the statute, but since I am the president, I can delegate a brother to start the meeting››.

A game of tennis well played by both competitors.

‹‹ I gladly accept the invitation››.

Redemption days

‹‹ Not at all... indeed I owe it to you, given your seniority in the association,›› I replied, making a slight bow as a sign of condescension towards him. That gesture of respect had struck him very much, as it had made a breach in all the others, who emitted almost in unison a sigh of approval and relief. The atmosphere had calmed down, so to speak, and the meeting got into full swing with the initial speech of the 'president': ‹‹ Gentlemen, unfortunately, a lot of time has passed since we agreed on a demonstration worthy of our organization, an act that, as you know, we had to postpone for external causes. Our intent was and is to hit the immoral during their lousy national demonstration that would take place in the main streets of our beloved city. Because of some rifts within those pseudo-associations, and because of some strong remonstrances from high public figures, the event has been postponed but not canceled!›› the buzz of protest and disapproval from the room.

‹‹ Perhaps you would have preferred the cancellation instead of the suspension, but, I can tell you that from our point of view it is fine. We will have more time to organize the fireworks! We can't allow those perverts to destroy young minds by inculcating the notion that homosexuality is normal! Furthermore, we can't do that!›› he said, shouting the last thoughts and pounding his fists on the table.

Classic move to focus attention on himself and at the same time to charge the listeners, a tactic that has always worked great. The public began to heat up, those who began to shout insults against associations or people, those who launched death threats or called for the creation of hypothetical correction camps in which to lock them up, and other ridiculous gestures that had little human. At that point, he calmed them down and resumed his speech.

‹‹ From the reports of our infiltrators, we have found out that in the end, the demonstration will take place, but that they will join with the Negro monkey associations! So we will kill two birds with one stone!›› roar of applause for the 'president'.

Having received, from the informants, the official route of the demonstration, the assembly drew up a simple plan. The route developed in about 1.2 miles along the main streets until it ended in front of the town hall for the ritual speech of the various representatives of the associations that had joined. The explosive devices, five, would be placed near the stage and on the only escape routes and would explode simultaneously when the leaders' speeches began. All were remotely operated. The association would have taken a mild position against the demonstration with the classic press release and, at most, we would have staged a sit-in protest, a way to avoid (as much as possible) the umpteenth search of the headquarters. We had to act in the shadows. The old man had called that meeting a simple formal gesture everything was already ready for the demonstrative action, the explosive devices had already been packed by our experts and placed in some safe warehouse in the city.

Redemption days

Suddenly one stood up and said, ‹‹ Gentlemen. I would like to propose a new agenda if I may››. Everyone turned in the direction of the voice, casting curious glances at each other.

‹‹ I don't think there's any problem, but it's up to the president to decide.››
‹‹ No problem,›› I replied calmly.
‹‹ I ask all of you for justice for our brother and his family, who recently passed away. His death must be avenged!››
‹‹ Justice? Yes, but in what way?››
‹‹ Yes... you're right. We must take revenge!›› Everyone was on the trail of revenge, and at that point, I understood that the old man wanted to frame me.
‹‹ We have to kill that bastard!›› Said one of them angrily. The bastard was none other than James.
‹‹ Wasn't he killed?››
‹‹ No. John thought he had been killed, but I know from reliable sources that he was saved!››.

The discussion resumed and thus: ‹‹ I'll take care of everything, don't worry. John will be avenged!››

At that sentence, thunderous applause of approval broke out towards me and some of those pigs dared to get up and come towards me to congratulate me on the decision. I had anticipated it. Surely he would have asked some of them to put my name forward, in the vain hope of my hesitation or refusal, which would have made me look even worse in front of the other members, but instead, I accepted the challenge. The only solution is to save our lives. From that moment on, I would be controlled day and night by his henchmen. The meeting could be said to be over and so everyone took the way home, except for yours truly who first leaped the dungeon of the association. I found myself in front of the mysterious box and unlike the first time, I had with me a good hammer with which to break the lock. I had decided to check the contents and leave the box, I didn't want any more trouble. Two well-timed blows and it opened without much trouble, but I must say I was quite disappointed by the contents. Just an old and worn military blanket and some letters tied together with string. I took a quick look at them before making them disappear inside my jacket and hiding the box again, and then headed for the exit and back home. I would read them later at my leisure.

Once I returned, I put that correspondence in the kitchen cupboard and I devoted myself to preparing something to eat in front of the television while I enjoyed the cable channel 47 where they broadcast 24 h on 24 h sports of all kinds. Eventually, tiredness got the better of me and I fell asleep in front of the television, and after a good hour or so, I woke up from that torpor and went to my room to resume sleeping.

Redemption days

When you're not looking for trouble, it's a trouble that visits you... even in the office! She had her secretary announce herself on that cold and rainy morning. She appeared at the door and with a polite manner warned me of an unscheduled visit and while I was about to tell her that I didn't want to be disturbed, he appeared with that sly smile of a son of a bitch and made his triumphant entrance, to the embarrassment of the secretary and my anger.

He said: ‹‹ Go ahead, no problem, thank you›› and I waved for him to sit down. ‹‹ Remember that in less than five minutes you have to go to that meeting. If you want...››

‹‹ Tell me yourself, please››. After so many years, that woman knew how to get me out of trouble. He didn't bother much, so he seemed at ease, almost the master. He sat down on the couch, carefully avoiding the two chairs in front of my desk, and said: ‹‹ Great taste in furniture››.
‹‹ Thank you, unfortunately, it is not my work, but you must miss me since you can't stay too long without seeing me!››
‹‹ I didn't think you were funny,›› he said, taking a quick look around the studio.
‹‹ A quality I keep hidden. To what do I owe this unexpected visit anyway?››

‹‹ What a hurry to send me away. You're not much of a visitor. Not even a cup of coffee? We're off to a bad start, you know››. Hot coffee in the face... bastard! I thought to myself, as I was about to pour him a cup.

‹‹ Now that I have behaved like an excellent guest, could you explain the reason for the visit? You know I have very little time left... the meeting...››. He remained silent, sipping his drink with gusto and slowly casting his gaze in every corner of the study. I said nothing and continued to observe him until my secretary (punctual as a Swiss watch) appeared to remind me of the 'phantom' meeting.

‹‹ I'm sorry to disturb you, but it's two minutes before the start of...››

‹‹ Thank you››.

‹‹ The report to be submitted is ready, would you like to check it to see if it is in order before I go to take the 'Morrison' file to the audit office?››

‹‹ No problem. It's all right, I'll go now. Thank you.››

Redemption days

‹‹ OK, whatever you say. See you later. See you later. Goodbye›› and went towards the revision office on the upper floor. At that moment, he got up from the couch and handed me the empty cup he went towards the door, stopping on the threshold. He turned to me and with a calm manner said: ‹‹ Nice test of courage, that of last night, and, by the way, remember to put back what you took before you hurt yourself›› and left me there open-mouthed, like a fool. That son of a bitch, he knew about the petty theft, and I could hardly believe it. The old man had come on purpose to warn me, to let me know that he knew everything and that he and only he commanded our lives, both inside and outside the association. What to do at that point? I wouldn't have deviated one inch from my intentions, also because James' life was at stake and I couldn't leave him at the mercy of their attentions, just as I certainly wouldn't have returned the money I had stolen, so, I would have put it in a safe place. All that interest rang a bell, perhaps I had found something to use against him. I remained holed up in my office, sitting in my chair contemplating nothing, while my mind was sifting through the possible moves.

‹‹ Excuse me, may I come in?››

‹‹ Sorry, I was distracted. I didn't hear you come in, go ahead››.

‹‹ I just had to tell you that the Morrison file is being examined by the revision office and that it will be sent to the head office within two days. Everything OK?››

‹‹ Everything is fine, thank you. Too much work...››

‹‹ Forgive me for this lack, the guest from before, had something sinister. I don't want to offend you...››

‹‹No offense.››

‹‹ No offense and you're not the only one who thinks so›› and I sketched a half-smile.

‹‹ You should do me a favor before you go.››

‹‹ What is it?››

‹‹ I need you to get me all the information on the new hire, the internship boy.››

‹‹ James?››

‹‹ That's him... isn't he back at work yet?››

‹‹ Not yet, she is still on sick leave. Would you like me to make copies of your personnel file?››

‹‹ Yes, I need them by the morning if it's not too much trouble.››

‹‹ You'll have the records by lunchtime.››

‹‹ Thank you››. Once I had the information, I had the secretary call him. If I had called him directly, he would have recognized both my cell phone and the private number of the office and, for sure, would not have answered.

‹‹ Hello?››

‹‹ James doesn't hang up, you're in danger! Listen to me... please...››

‹‹ Curious... the big pussy-busting man who has a third person call a pussy for lack of assholes!››

‹‹ He wants you dead! And he will hunt you down until he kills you!››

‹‹ I'm not afraid. I will know how to react, so you can go back to your miserable life and remember what we said to each other in the cemetery››

‹‹ I remember well what you told me, but for fuck's sake... give me a chance to save your ass! Goddamn fucking kid! Do you think you're gonna be a hero? Use your goddamn brain and get some help... you know as well as I do, those guys don't mess around! Then you can tell me to fuck off!››

Redemption days

‹‹ Tomorrow night, 10:00 pm., Desert Hill, 8th Street. No jokes. I won't be alone or helpless like the first time!››.

The first problem had been 50% solved, assuming the boy had listened to me at that meeting. Now I had to find a safe hiding place for the stolen goods, but first I was going to cover my back by photocopying the letters that I, fortunately, had with me. I decided to make two copies that I would hide in different places: one in a safe deposit box in my bank and the second I would give to my secretary to be put in the safe of the company and both would be accompanied by a letter with instructions on what to do with them, in case something serious happened to me.

On the night of the meeting, I took a cab to 8th Street and got out in front of the club, but as I got out, I heard the driver make a not-so-subtle comment about me: 'you fucking cocksucker! For the first time in my life, I was judged with the same contempt and standard of judgment that I had used myself until some time before. I paid for the ride by giving him a mischievous smile to mock him, to which he reacted with a disgusted face, speeding off towards his next destination. Curiously, he hated gays, not their money! The big luminous sign with two male symbols joined together and the name of the club underneath illuminated by day left nothing to the imagination about the type of clientele. The bouncer in charge of guarding the entrance and the line of people waiting to get in, behind the barriers with velvet ropes, made me realize that the place was 'IN' and classy. Diligently I positioned myself in the line, waiting for James, who had not yet arrived. There were still three people ahead of me, then I could get in, but I kept looking around in vain for James. It was almost half an hour after 10 pm, so I called his cell phone... one... two... three... four rings, then it went to voicemail. I closed the communication, leaving no message. Once inside, I was met by a waiter who led the way to a table. I ordered a dry martini and tried to reach James again.

Nothing. Even though the bars on his cell phone indicated the greatest level of reception, he didn't answer. In the end, I decided to wait and enjoy the evening, maybe he had had a last-minute setback... and then I warned him to be careful.

Redemption days

‹‹ Excuse me, are you waiting for James?›› I turned around and saw the closet acting as a bouncer all smiles. I just stared at him like an idiot, not answering yes or no to his question.

‹‹ I'm sorry, small mistake of person.››

‹‹ No mistake... excuse me... the person you're looking for is me, my pleasure››.

‹‹ How do you do? I can only stay for half an hour, then I will have to take my place at the entrance. Let's call each other››.

‹‹ OK. Listen... but has James shown up?››

‹‹ No, why?››

‹‹ We had an appointment at 22, but ...››

‹‹ Too late, and that's not like him.››

‹‹ No calls or texts, but I called him on his cell phone, but it always goes to voicemail››.

‹‹ Maybe he's on his way, I'm going now... in case you know where to find me›› and he greeted me with a squeeze that made my fingers crunch. Beep! Beep! Beep! A text message. The number was the boy's, finally. Possibly he was on his way... and: 'Your little woman is in good hands! Three days and you'll know where to show up, mind you, no tricks!'. I hurriedly headed for the exit and asked his friend if he could step away from his post for a few minutes, it was an emergency. The man didn't ask twice, called one of his colleagues through the microphone, and we moved to a private office inside the club.

‹‹ No one will bother us here. It's James, isn't it?››

‹‹ The boy is in very serious trouble...›› I didn't have time to finish the sentence when I found myself lying on the floor with a split lip.

‹‹ Dirty bastard!››.

In the fall, I dragged with me a crystal table that went in shattered. The beast came at me with a chair to smash it on my head and at that point, I yelled at him to stop, that if he killed me, James would die! At that point, he threw the chair aside and said in a threatening tone: ‹‹ Two minutes of time››. That's all I needed to convince him of my good faith. ‹‹ I know the guy who took him hostage. We can't notify the authorities, otherwise, he'll kill him, and I can assure you that he's a man who keeps his promises... If you want to save him, you'll have to cooperate with me, even if you hate me, otherwise...››.

Without saying anything, he left me in the office alone, still on the floor licking my wounds. He immediately returned with two bottles of beer, took the overturned chair, and arranged himself in front of me, stretching me one of the two beers that I grabbed without a word.

‹‹ I took the whole night off, now tell me everything you know, and don't make me regret leaving you in one piece!››.

He was already aware of the entire issue of my involvement in the beating, the betrayal, and also the reason for the meeting, so I told him about the meeting that took place at the association and the last meeting I had with the old man. Furthermore, he listened attentively and then got up and gave me a business card saying: ‹‹ I'll give you a hand to save him, but I warn you, don't play games with me, or I'll kill you!›› and pointed to the door.

On the way out, I found a cab ready to take me home.

Redemption days

Three days of searching, of waiting. Three long days of figuring out where she was keeping him hidden. Her country house! That's where! A secluded place, safe and almost unknown to most. I took the business card and read the phone number... Drin! Drin! Drin! "Damn the phone! Just when I needed it!" I thought, annoyed. I answered a little pissed off and on the other side, I recognized Michael's voice, a young novice follower but, if I remember correctly, very close to the leader. The storm was coming over our heads, and it would be the storm of the century. I thanked him for the call and as soon as I was done with him, I called the living closet. He gave me an appointment around 2 pm when the place was closed and warned me that he would not be alone but that no one would put their hands on me. Besides myself and Joseph, I found seven other people who looked at me with inquiring eyes full of anger. I avoided digressions and went straight to the question: «You could only keep him, prisoner, in two places. His main house and the country house. I think it is more likely to be the country house, but I have to find out the address and I also know where to find the information».

Joseph asked me: «When can you tell us the information?»

«Tomorrow morning, via text message. One last thing before going: you must stop the demonstration! You must not postpone it... you must cancel it!»

«I don't think we can do it.»

«Do it, otherwise there will be more innocent deaths!»

«Attack? Your friends have prepared an attack?».

I nodded, and then all hell broke loose. Two tried to attack me, and fortunately for me, Joseph kept his promise to me on the phone. It took a while before calm returned and I could resume speaking: ‹‹ Listen to me, you have to cancel it››.

‹‹ Listen, but if the event were to be canceled out of the blue, wouldn't they get suspicious?››.

Yeah, I hadn't thought of that.

‹‹ Then you could postpone it until James is released, and then we'll sound the alarm. Remember, there are also spies inside››.

‹‹ Spies now? I think this guy's taking the piss.››

‹‹ In fact, he's a double agent.››

‹‹ The organization is very powerful and little by little it has branched out into all levels and even within you. Let's free James, and then we'll think about dismantling it! The information is inside the association, so tonight I'll be able to send it to you by SMS, so you can free the boy before the ultimatum expires. So?››

‹‹ You've convinced me and I think the others will agree too. Let me know as soon as you find something, and then we'll do some cleanup.››.

Joseph shook my hand and accompanied me to the exit of the club.

‹‹ We'll be waiting to hear from you.››

‹‹ OK. Then I'll join you to give you a hand... even if as a soldier I'm not worth anything!››

Redemption days

‹‹ Two more hands are always handy››.

After visiting the club, I stopped by the office to retrieve the information, useful to the liberation commando. I went straight to the office and wondered if I'd found him there sitting behind the desk with that evil grin of his branded on his face, ready to greet me. No unpleasant surprises, but I could feel his presence. He had left some of his personal belongings in plain sight to remind me who was in charge, like a god who came down to earth and became a man with the mission of creating an Aryan world. He could at least open the window when he finished smoking his disgusting cigar, damn him. I ventilated the room then I started looking for information, I could not find anything on paper but on the PC I would find what I was looking for. I did a quick check and after a few minutes, I managed to find the sensitive data of the current members, including those of the old man, with two addresses for a house in town and one outside. Furthermore, I sent the address to Joseph and turned off the PC to reach them, my mission within the association was over.

The pain, in the back of my neck, was throbbing like a jackhammer. It took a few minutes for my eyes to adjust to the darkness around me and figure out where I was. I was not in the office of the association. I tried to touch myself with my right hand at the point where I had received the blow, but I couldn't reach it, because my wrists and ankles were tied with chains, fixed to the wall. Short, new, strong chains. Luckily, I wasn't standing up – that had been spared. The room was small, damp, dirty, and without any windows, and the only opening was the door in front of me, firmly closed. The room must have been underground, a sort of cellar, and I hoped it was the house where the liberation commando would have broken into, but with my luck, I had got the wrong house. The air exchange was provided by an old forced-air unit, which must have been in full operation for a long time. Since I couldn't run away (my I-phone had been taken away) and it certainly wasn't visiting hours, I tried to recreate in my mind the events before the blow to the head.

After turning off the PC, I got up to go close the window with my back to the door, and... what an asshole! There had to be at least two of them to transport me to the prison. James was not in that cellar, and maybe not even in that house, or maybe he was already at liberty to celebrate with his friends the escaped danger... yes, they had freed him... I was sure of it... or so I hoped. Let's go! Bastard! What the fuck do you want from me? Tell me!" I shouted to the empty room. I felt like I was in the movie 'Saw -The Riddler' but I didn't need to wait until the end of the movie to understand who was behind it all.

‹‹ I bet you set up some CCTV cameras to watch me and have fun, right? Show up and face me like a man! Grow a pair of balls!››.

Redemption days

Just the fact of insulting and provoking him freed my soul from a big burden. I stayed there for a few hours, and maybe I fell asleep because suddenly I heard a voice calling my name. A voice I knew. In front of me, a shadow materialized and gradually got closer and closer to me, until it became clearer, and I noticed that he was wearing a black hood that hid his entire face, and he was carrying a bottle and a cloth.

I had time to see a few drops of the contents of the bottle fall before I lost consciousness again. Chloroform. The good little soldier had completed the mission he had been assigned, that is to transfer me to another point of the house.

I awoke a few hours later (perhaps he had overdosed on chloroform), bound hand and foot to a chair, in the center of a well-lit and very tastefully decorated room. A study with a library and expensive, period furniture. In front of me were a solid fir desk and a leather armchair with a huge back. On the wall behind the desk, there was a painting of exaggerated dimensions even for a gallery and the subject... Him! Portrayed at the top of a hill with his chest out like a frog in the act of frightening his enemy, his hands on his hips, and his proud and hard look with his 'unforgettable' demonic grin on his face. The clothes... he should have sued his designer! The uniform he wore must have been a hybrid inspired by Goering's gaudy uniforms or those of the U.S. Army, and he certainly could not miss the 'famous' beam of divine light that consecrated him as the messiah of the salvation of mankind! A tacky painting!

I was waiting for his triumphant entrance into the room, but I was disappointed to see his trusted soldier enter, all happy to have accomplished his mission. Rusty. The right person for that kind of work.

‹‹ Good morning, little princess cocksucker!›› he smiled. A little boy full of complexes, eyes not very bright in a face from which shone his total ignorance and arrogance. His only strength was his size, added to the muscles that he cultivated between the various gyms and small illegal wrestling matches in which he participated every weekend, earning good money (when he won) and many wounds of which he was proud as if they were medals won for military valor. Observing more carefully, he didn't give me the impression of a womanizer, and maybe he paid for a few seconds of pleasure. A 'yes-man' with a small penis complex, sexually impotent, and prone to brawling and sadism. A person you would avoid any kind of relationship with, even the mere exchange of glances. He would walk in front of me, pacing back and forth, stopping occasionally to cast me glances devoid of humanity and intelligence. I knew he had a crazy desire to kill me with his bare hands, but the plans were different, and he had to respect them, even if he was getting more and more nervous.

At that point, I decided to break the silence: ‹‹ Rusty, my friend, relax.››

‹‹ Don't call me a friend. I'm not friends with a dirty faggot!›› he replied altered.

‹‹ You go around being nice to other people, and you're swamped with shit!››

‹‹ In your position, I would avoid being funny!››

‹‹ And what situation am I in, pray to tell?››

Redemption days

‹‹ Shut your fucking mouth, you lousy asshole!››

I avoided going any further and remained silent. Rusty was nervously looking at his watch while simultaneously glancing in the direction of the door as if he was waiting for someone late, and it didn't take a genius to figure out that the person in question was the old puppet master. Suddenly he got up from the chair, in which he had before sat, dropped it to the floor, and disappeared, leaving me alone in the room. Very impulsive boy and not very patient. While waiting, I tried to loosen the ropes on my wrists, but nothing. Tied up like a salami! I could feel the rubbing of the nylon rope tearing my skin with every vain attempt. I gritted my teeth but continued the operation, even if it meant sawing off my wrists.

‹‹ Do you need a hand?›› at that question, I looked up and saw him standing in front of me.
‹‹ Shut your mouth if you don't want to eat flies for breakfast››. I was speechless. He stood behind me and, with a quick gesture, cut the ropes that held me, prisoner, to the chair, then helped me up. My legs were still slightly numb from lack of circulation, and I found it difficult to walk, but there wasn't much time, so... pain or not, I walked towards the exit and salvation.

When we left the house we found ourselves in the garden and, without thinking twice, we started to run in the direction of the main gate and once over, not without some difficulty, we moved away from that villa. The street we were running along was lined on both sides with villas surrounded by greenery with high walls, gates, and cameras placed at every corner of their fences. 'Kensington!'

A piece of old England in the American heartland was built four years ago! I had read a few articles and followed the details of television from its design to its completion. Kensington' was nothing more than a sort of private paradise for the vacations of the country's rich, who wanted to retreat to protected areas with a different level of privacy, if I remember correctly, the whole area was surrounded by massive walls and there was only one access road guarded by well-trained and armed private security agents. I pointed this out to my fellow escapee, who remained calm and confident in his actions. I followed him like a puppy on the deserted main street, we didn't cross a soul, not even surveillance cars or dog walkers.

Redemption days

No one was chasing us, and I was very worried about that. We turned right towards 'Road Kensington', leaving the main road. About ten feet down the road, we turned left, so we went down that road for a few feet, then left again... and finally found ourselves at a dead-end. We ended our escape in front of a boundary wall, several meters high and quite thick. From his trouser pocket he took out some sort of credit card, which turned out to be an electronic key, and he approached a large bush of climbing ivy, began to rummage through it, and... A door materialized before my eyes with an electronic box with a red light that turned green when he swiped the card in the slot and as if by magic, the door opened wide to freedom. I confess that I watched in disbelief mixed with admiration for his inventiveness. He was no rookie! James had amazed me to no end.

‹‹ Cell phone?›› I asked James.

He looked me straight in the eye and nodded no: "You?".

‹‹ No››. They had taken the necessary precautions. Good or bad I knew where we were, not exactly the exact point Google Maps style, but I could trace the direction to take to reach the city and raise the alarm. Our priority was to find the highway as soon as possible to hitchhike back home. Now the roles were reversed. I had become the guide, while James was following me confidently. Almost three hours passed before we saw a busy road with the roaring sound of cars whizzing along with the asphalt in both directions. The sun had set, and soon darkness took the place of light. At that point no one would have stopped to pick up two cold and hungry hitchhikers, so the idea of spending the night out in the cold was becoming concrete, as much as it was damned unpleasant, but with no cash, no credit cards, and no cell phones, that remained our only option. When we reached the edge of the road, we rested for a few minutes, sitting on the ground and watching the cars speeding past us.

‹‹ James, how are you? The arm?›› I asked him worried about his condition.
‹‹ My arm still hurts, but I'm fine. How about you? You look like a zombie!››
‹‹ I may be tired, but I can handle it. But what do we do now? Any ideas?››.

He stared at me with his tired but lively eyes and answered: ‹‹ We'll spend the night in that small motel›› and pointed at the luminous sign 'free rooms' then he resumed: ‹‹ Tomorrow morning we'll go back to the city, and we'll see what to do with all the others››. All the others, yeah... but which ones?

‹‹ I don't think they'll be available yet, considering how things went.››
‹‹ What happened?››.

Redemption days

At that point, I explained the situation and the trap we had fallen into. The boy was speechless. He didn't want to believe it, he got up from the ground and covered his face with his hands, he was crying with rage. I tried to reassure him about the fate of his friends, after all the real target was us and not them. I went next to him and with a paternal attitude, I hugged him, wrapping him in a warm and protective embrace.

‹‹ Thank you. I needed that››
‹‹ Thanks to you for saving me!››.

I shrugged my shoulders and gave him a light pat on the shoulder, then he pointed me to continue to the motel. When we reached the entrance, I had a slight doubt. I blocked him with my hand and asked him in a low voice: ‹‹ How do you plan to pay the bill?››.

No money, no room!

He smiled and entered with confidence. The girl at the counter greeted us cheerfully and began to list the comforts of the rooms. Single, double, twin, and all with telephone, television, private bathroom and if we wanted something to eat, she had a large selection of sandwiches and drinks at reasonable prices. No free double rooms, and given the prices of singles and doubles, James preferred the last alternative. He also ordered a few sandwiches and two bottles of water, paying in cash. The girl went to take the food and the key to the room and then say the way to reach it.

‹‹ Good boy! You managed to hide a few green cards... congratulations.››

‹‹ After the last lightning in the subway, I had to organize››.

Room number 12. Clean and comfortable.

‹‹ If you want to go to the bathroom first, do not make compliments››.

‹‹ Thank you, I must confess I need it. Two minutes!››

‹‹ Take your time. In the meantime I will watch some television and, if I am lucky, I will be able to find a sports channel››.

I turned on the television and did some zapping, but I wasn't looking for sports, I was looking for a local channel to watch a new program. Maybe I was expecting some half-baked news announcing the start of the hunt for two fugitives from the residential center after a failed robbery attempt, but no news of that sort, so I finally stopped on 57, where they were broadcasting a football game. James came out of the bathroom with a more relaxed face and apologized for taking so long. Instead of two minutes, he had been in the bathroom for almost fifteen minutes. Let's just say he'd taken it pretty easy. A refresher would have cheered me up and calmed the tension of the last few events.

After having dinner in front of the television, tiredness took over, and so we decided to get under the covers with a slight embarrassment on my part. Sharing a double bed with another man who was also homosexual made me uncomfortable and to lighten the mood he let himself go to a joke: ‹‹ Don't get any ideas, you're not my type!››.

Redemption days

"That statement tore me an amused smile for that situation was all new to me."

In the darkness of the room, the initial sleep decided to make itself wanted and only by me. James asked if we would be able to save ourselves or if we would be killed trying to escape. I couldn't answer him. In my heart, I didn't know how it would end, then he asked me to make him a promise. If everything went well, I would have to commit to making peace with Lorelain. Which was impossible.

‹‹ James, I can't promise you that. The marriage is ruined now.››
‹‹ Maybe the marriage, but not the relationships. After all, you're still in love with her and so is she. All you have to do is talk to her from the heart, as I advised you to do in the club.››

Yeah, the advice I hadn't followed, and now it was too late to turn back. Maybe it had to be like that, and I couldn't change the past, but the boy didn't take no for an answer.

‹‹ You also have to show her that you have changed. This will make you see yourself in a different light, and I'm sure when it's all over, your life will pick up where it left off. I can feel it.››
I don't.

‹‹ I ask your forgiveness for all the bad things I've done to you. That time in the cemetery... you didn't give me a chance... and you had every reason to!››

‹‹ I hated your guts. I wanted to kill you with my own hands! I miss her! We loved each other very much, and maybe we would have been able to spend all our lives together, unfortunately, he will never come back. I miss him!››

‹‹ Why didn't you report me to the police? Why the fuck didn't you take revenge? You could have even asked your friends for help and had me slaughtered as I did to you... why didn't you do any of that? Why?››

‹‹ By turning yourself in you would have only been the one to pay while the real mastermind would have gotten away with it and then, have you beaten to a pulp? I'm not a coward who makes others do the dirty work. And...››

‹‹ And what?››

‹‹ Nothing. Now let's get some sleep, we have a hard day ahead of us tomorrow. Good night.››

Too convenient to cut the conversation short to avoid answering me.

‹‹ Give me one reason for your behavior››.

I turned on the light and got out of bed, standing in front of him, still under the sheets. He was staring at the ceiling, and a slight tremor in his hand revealed a hidden tension.

‹‹ You were used, is that enough motivation for you?››

‹‹ I know full well that I was used. The old bastard arranged everything, but you didn't tell all it. You can tell a mile away that you're holding on to a big, oppressive weight. Get rid of it, come on!›› I said, approaching him and sitting on the edge of the bed. He turned his face away and finally said.

Redemption days

‹‹ My grandfather!››.

That revelation was like a punch in the gut.

‹‹ When he became a widower, he decided to move to another city to change the air and forget the pain of losing his grandmother. He only showed up for the holidays, for the rest of the year, he disappeared and was rarely heard from, even by phone. I can tell you that he had a fragmented and detached relationship with us, but when we needed help, he would miraculously appear out of nowhere. He didn't have financial problems he had plenty of money and I honestly don't remember how he made his fortune, but his mind was rather bigoted, narrow-minded, and racist... and I suppose you noticed that too, right?››

Let's say that I had slightly sensed it, but just slightly.

‹‹ Her wish was to make me her heir, having had only two girls and no male grandchildren other than myself, the choice had fallen on me. Two days after Christmas, I must have been about eight years old, he took me to a shopping mall, just to take a walk and spend some time in each other's company. I held his hand as we walked through the large spaces of the mall, and now and then he would stop to look at some of the display cases, and the only thing he bought was a bag full of gummy candies and as an extra a lollipop. He chose that, while the bag of candy was my choice. Perhaps to overdo it a little in my eyes, he decided on the biggest and most colorful lollipop of all those on display in the store. Everything at that time seemed enormous to me, after all, I was observing with the eyes of a child. While I was waiting for him outside the door of the toilets, a black boy approached me, a little younger than me, shyly asked me for a treat. I didn't have time to give it to him, but from behind, I heard his hoarse voice admonishing me not to give the candy to that little nigger. The child ran away in tears from fright. He grabbed me by the arm and dragged me towards the exit of the mall with such a fury that it hurt. In my haste, I lost all the sweets, including the lollipop that fell to the ground and broke into four pieces, and at that point I began to cry, begging him to let go of my arm. He was adamant, he had to teach me a lesson. On the way back, the dear grandfather gave me a detailed lesson on racism against African-Americans, Jews, homosexuals, and all other categories considered inferior and dangerous to the supremacy of the white Aryan race›› he took a breath.

He motioned me to move from the edge of the bed and stood up. He went in front of the window and, removing the curtain, resumed the story.

Redemption days

‹‹ From that day on, he worked hard to get his thoughts into my head, to make me like him. Are you wondering about my parents' reaction? Well, they did nothing to prevent Grandpa's brainwashing. They did not openly and publicly approve of grandfather's thinking, but deep down they believed in it and how. I didn't say anything about what happened at the mall, I kept everything inside, and that night, alone in my room, I cried my heart out. I was afraid that they would hear me and punish me for what they considered a weakness. Furthermore, I'll let you imagine how I spent my childhood and adolescence. It sucked terribly! When he heard about my homosexuality, he went on a rampage. And in my opinion, he was the one who organized my forced hospitalization in that damn clinic. When I managed to escape, he sent me a message: 'You won't be able to escape for long. I will catch you and avenge the good name of my family that you have stained with your abomination!' I was terrified of what he would do to me if he caught me, fortunately, I found many people who gave me protection and help››.

And some of them betrayed you like a Judas.

‹‹ He used the association he founded and the high connections to tool the plan. Having discovered the relationship with Arthur, son of an active member of the association and your close friend, at that point Grandpa arranged for me to get a job right in your company to use as pawns. Chess is his favorite game, and he can play it very well in real life too, but unfortunately, something went wrong. The destabilizing factor was you!›› he said in a proud tone.

I was the destabilizing factor of his revenge? How could it be?

‹‹ He had not calculated the human factor. Even if it was a delayed outburst, you repented and turned against him.››

The old man thought of leaving me in charge of the association, maybe he thought I was strong and worthy of his trust and that I would remain at his side during the battle, unfortunately, he didn't take into account the human factor towards the boy and the tragic death of my dear friend and his family, which radically changed the way I saw the world around me. He now found himself having to drop both his nephew and me, and would not stop until he had achieved his goal.

‹‹ Good night›› James said, tucking himself under the covers.

Redemption days

I said nothing. I remained silent and lay down beside him. Likewise, I turned off the light and we both tried to get to sleep, even though it was difficult. The next morning I got up before the sun came up, I'd only been asleep for a few hours anyway, I'd spent the rest of the night thinking about how to get out of it. James was still asleep, I could hear his regular breathing, maybe he too had fallen asleep late, I decided not to disturb him and got up to go to the bathroom to freshen up. I stood in front of the sink with only the mirror lights on and continued to stare at myself in disbelief. I knew that that reflection was me, but at the same time, I was seeing another person. Deep, black circles under his eyes, a lean, scarred face with a three-day beard. The eyes are considered the mirror of the soul, dull and empty. No sign of vitality. The will to fight was slowly waning and then, would we have been able to beat him? None of us could have, at that point, withdrawn from the race for salvation, he would have prevented it. Thoughts to chase away, damn it!

‹‹ Let's freshen up and go out and enjoy a good breakfast!›› I said to the reflected image.

The rest would come later. Thinking on a full stomach was another matter. After all, I had never thought clearly in the early morning, except after a cup of bitter black coffee.

As soon as I got out of the bathroom, I saw James sitting on the bed, cross-legged and wide awake, watching some television. The boy had turned into a music channel, where they were broadcasting the video clip of the band of the moment. It was a screaming song (close to metal) with lyrics devoid of any logical sense but strangely catchy. From the rhythmic head and hand movement, James liked it.

‹‹ Get up from that bed lazybones and come wash, then we go to breakfast››.

He stared at me with those blue eyes and smiling he went to the bathroom singing the chorus of that song, and honestly, I had never heard anyone singing out of tune in that terrible way.
‹‹ We can go to the diner next door, I don't think we're going to be depleted alive,›› he said as he finished dressing in his clothes from the day before.

‹‹ How many dollars do we have in the cash register?››
‹‹ Let me check... let's see... about 15 bucks. It will also be enough to buy bus tickets back to the city. What time do we have to vacate the room?››
‹‹ By 11, so after we eat we also have time to freshen up, of course, if you hurry!››
‹‹ I'm ready... I'm ready, let's go, come on!››

The diner was right in front of our motel and to our surprise, we met the girl who was at the front desk, the night of our arrival.

‹‹ Hello. What can I get you good?››

Redemption days

‹‹ How come you work here too?››

The diner was right in front of our motel and to our surprise, we met the girl who was at the front desk the night we arrived.

‹‹ Hello. What can I get you good?››

‹‹ How come you work here too?›› asked James.

‹‹ Excuse him for his intrusiveness. Too curious.››

‹‹ No problem. I work from time to time when I'm not at college. Both the motel and the diner belong to my parents.››

Has your curiosity been satisfied?

‹‹Yes››.

I noticed a slight blush appearing on the boy's face. I had embarrassed him.

‹‹ I recommend the 'home-cooked breakfast' consisting of eggs, bacon, toast, and a choice of a cup of coffee or orange juice for the modest sum of $8.50 for two orders.››

‹‹ We accept the suggestion, but I would prefer the squeezed version and for the old man here in front of me, I believe the one with the coffee cup, or am I wrong?››

‹‹ No mistake, thank you››

‹‹ I will bring your orders in a few minutes, drinks in a second››

‹‹ Thank you, take your time, we're in no hurry.››

We didn't look like a couple of fugitives, not really. We looked like a father and son on a men-only outing, even though our clothes and faces might suggest the idea of escape. Furthermore, we were enjoying those quiet moments before we jumped back into the fray.

‹‹ Here are your drinks: coffee and orange juice. The rest is in preparation.››

‹‹ Thank you.››

‹‹ Any other requests?›› asked the girl.

‹‹ Listen, could you fetch me a copy of today's paper, if you can and if you don't mind?››

‹‹ I think so, but you won't find much about last night's attacks in New York. In case, I can turn on the radio for you.››

At that news, James and I turned white. The girl told us that shortly before four o'clock in the morning, New Yorkers were awakened by the roar of six bombs exploded in different parts of the city. There were innocent victims in the collapse of two buildings on the outskirts of the city, while in the other episodes there was only damage to buildings. The targets seemed to have been the associations for the struggle for civil rights, gays, and African-Americans, so the investigators had pointed the finger at the far-right movements. No claim had been received, and perhaps it would never come. The old bastard had given the okay for the operation, and they certainly hadn't spared themselves in using explosives. Dirty bastards! James barely touched his breakfast: the anger at that news had closed his stomach.

Redemption days

‹‹ Damn it! I can't think about this! I get a rage... Fuck!››

‹‹ He can't help it, when he puts his mind to something, that bastard accomplishes it.››

‹‹ Yes, but this time he did it to set you up.››

‹‹ Yeah, that's what I thought. After all, I'm the head of the association that carried out the attacks, but the authorities haven't...››

‹‹ Lookout... in front of the motel.›› James pointed to the exact spot and I saw them getting out of the black car, parked right there in front.

‹‹ You think cops or feds?››

‹‹ Worse...››

‹‹ They?››

‹‹ Members of his gang. We have got to run, let's go!›› and we got up from the table, where our freshly touched plates still stood.

I didn't know what the fuck to do! I was panicking. Even if we had managed to get out of the club, how were we going to escape? On foot? James asked Julia to point us to the back exit of the diner, and so he led us through the kitchen and into the loading and unloading area of the diner. A sort of dirt parking lot with a pickup truck and a hatchback parked out front.

‹‹ Take my car, here are the keys,›› he offered generously and unexpectedly.

‹‹ We thank you...how did you figure it out?››

‹‹ You are not the first fugitives to pass through these parts, but I can tell you that you are the first to whom I entrust my car for escape››.

‹‹ Aren't you afraid of being charged with aiding and abetting?››

‹‹ I don't have a problem, and besides, I'm sure those two henchmen who are looking for you are not agents or am I mistaken?››

She was not mistaken.

‹‹ Now go, or they will catch you!››
‹‹ Thank you from the bottom of my heart... and we will try to treat her well and make sure you find her. I promise!››
‹‹ Thank you, Julia!››
‹‹ Now go... it's that green hope!›› I watched her slowly disappear from the rear-view mirror.

Smart girl with balls! Damn!

I didn't take the direction to town, but decided on a second chance, hoping to remember the exact route to get there. James, by my side, wouldn't stop looking back and if he spotted the black car, he would warn me. After an hour of driving, he put his mind at ease, calmed down, and took in the view through the window. I took a dirt road, raising clouds of dust and dirt, and after some time stopped in front of a wooden house.

‹‹ Let's get off, we'll be safe here.›› He said nothing and walked to the entrance.

Redemption days

At the same time, I took the car to the other side of the building to hide it from prying eyes, even though we were in open country, the area was a holiday resort and sometimes a few cars could pass by. James did not move and when he saw me he said: ‹‹ Are we sure?››

I nodded in the affirmative. I picked up a stone from the patio of the house and, turning it over, extracted the entrance key. They hadn't changed the hiding place for the spare key, even after my complaints, but at that point, I thought it was better that way, otherwise, I would have had to break a window and my guests certainly wouldn't have taken it well.

‹‹ Make yourself comfortable, meanwhile I'm going to turn on the generator and the gas cylinder, so we won't miss the hot water and electricity. Then I'll think about preparing a meal.››
‹‹ Are you sure?››
‹‹ My boy, that's the second time you've asked me that, aren't you turning into a broken record? Try to relax, and lie down on the couch, make yourself at home››.
‹‹ I'm sorry, but when I'm under pressure, I happen to repeat sentences like a parrot. Now I lie down.››
‹‹ Try to rest, I know that the tension of these last days is killing us, but we have to hold on until the end››.

The electric generator was at the back, inside a small padlocked compartment, next to the LPG cylinder. I did everything I could to reactivate it and fortunately, everything went well. When I returned home, I noticed that James had fallen asleep on the couch, he couldn't stand the tension of his grandfather's surprise. I decided to let him rest, and in the meantime, I prepared something to eat. My former in-laws never forgot to stock the pantry with canned food, after they had once forgotten the supplies at home. At that time of year, the house wasn't used often and Lorelain's parents had also used it less and less; in the end, she and I hardly went there either. The place, beautiful, surrounded by vegetation with beautiful landscapes and sunsets, was too isolated: in the end, after having taken the classic walks in the woods and some fishing trips, you didn't know what to do anymore; you were fine for a few weekends, no more. Beans, dried meat, bottles of water and coffee, sugar, and dry biscuits, given the quantities we would not have risked starvation, also because we would have stopped at most for another two days to rest and decide what to do. I prepared some dried meat with a side of stewed beans and for dessert some crackers. Not exactly a delicacy. At that point, I woke him up and invited him to eat something, even though his stomach was still in knots, and I can tell you that he was not the only one in a precarious emotional state.

‹‹ So from what you've told me, we're at your in-laws' vacation home. Not a bad hiding place.››

‹‹ The only place I could think of to disappear for a few days.››

‹‹ No phone or TV, I see.››

Redemption days

‹‹ That's right. No technological devices around, when you came here, it was to be in close contact with nature and disconnect from the outside world to recharge your batteries.››

‹‹ A real bore!››

‹‹ Indeed... a real bore!›› and I laughed, amused.

James settled down in the guest room, while I took the master bedroom and, after a long time, slept in a familiar place. The next morning I got up early, after a quick shower, I decided to go out to make some wood for the fireplace, meanwhile, James had also got up, and serenely, he devoted himself to the preparation of breakfast. Splitting some logs would have helped me to discharge the last remnants of the accumulated tension. I took a few logs in my hands and entered the house and: ‹‹ We have some wood for the fireplace, so... what are you doing here?›› I said all surprised by that vision, making the logs fall to the ground, and I almost made them all fall on my feet.

‹‹ Actually, I'm the one who asked you, damn you!›› I remained silent and fortunately, James ran to retrieve me.

‹‹ I think it's time to explain the whole thing, reasonably. Let's go to the kitchen, and you'll get all the answers you deserve››.

She was the last person I thought I would meet in that isolated place. We sat around the table and James began to recount our story from the day we didn't meet in the club until that very moment. Lorelain listened attentively, casting looks of terror and disapproval at what she heard, and when James told her that her grandfather and the boss were the same people, she let out an expletive worthy of a longshoreman. At the end of the story, we both fell silent. She was still processing all those dramatic revelations in her mind. Suddenly I asked her why she had come.

‹‹ Why do you think?››
‹‹ I'm asking because I don't have the slightest idea.››
‹‹ Yesterday morning I received a call from your secretary, very concerned about your absence from work.›› Damn it! I had completely forgotten I had a job!

She couldn't reach you at home or on your cell phone, so she decided to call me and let me know her worries and doubts.

‹‹ I could have been sick and unable to call the office, couldn't I? It wouldn't have been the first time I had given a late notice››
‹‹ It would have been normal if she hadn't told me about the envelope you gave her to keep jealously in the company safe and the meeting with that bastard! Not to mention that James had also disappeared into thin air and then... damn you two! The attacks... that envelope to be kept, and the cell phone switched off... what was I supposed to think?››

Redemption days

‹‹ That we were up to our necks in shit and hiding, so you thought of the only known safe place. This cove, right?››

‹‹ Indeed... you bastard! I didn't know what happened to you, and I honestly didn't even know if you were still alive!›› She cried. I took her in my arms and held her against my chest.

‹‹ Forgive me for all the bad things I did to you but try to understand the situation. I didn't want to put your life in danger. I still love you madly!››

At that revelation, Lorelain released her grip and kissed me.

‹‹ The divorce was a mistake! I love you!›› A mistake that could have been repaired, if we had managed to stay alive.

‹‹ Sorry to interrupt your reconciliation, but we have other visitors,›› said James, pointing through the window to a black car that was coming.

Those bastards had discovered us! We had to run and take cover. I ordered both of us to go behind the house and get the car, we'd escape down the backstreets and onto the main road, hoping to lose our tracks. James took Lorelain's hand and led the way through the backyard, while I grabbed the car keys and bolted the door with the couch. It wouldn't have done much good, but I would have slowed them down, after all, they weren't expecting a getaway car.

The two goons didn't waste any time and started unloading their magazines on the door and the rest of the house. The windowpanes shattered to smithereens, and bullets started flying inside like rain. I dodged a few of them and finally rushed into the kitchen and then into the garden. Fortunately, the car was still open, so we got in, and the next thing I knew I saw them inside the house, so I put my foot on the accelerator and set off to get as far away from there as possible.

‹‹ Dear...were those gunshots I heard earlier? And who were those guys?››
‹‹ Lorelain, those guys are the old man's goons, and I honestly hope we get to the highway before they catch us because then I don't know what they'll do to us! And lastly, your parents are going to have to do a lot of repairs!››

The car was holding up well to the bumps in the road, and I could control it well enough to allow me to go at a high speed in the middle of that forest.

‹‹ James, check behind us to see if we're being followed.››
‹‹ No one in sight, just in case, don't worry.››
‹‹ Thanks kid, you're a legend! Lorelain, you alright?››
‹‹ I'm fine, just drive... Ahhhhh! Watch out for that overhanging branch!››.

I narrowly avoided it but it scratched the whole body, causing an unpleasant noise.

‹‹ Where are we going?››

Redemption days

‹‹ I hope it's the right way from the highway to the city, where we can call for help.››

‹‹ I trust you... and your instincts!›› We managed to get onto the entrance road when our lookout alerted us that we were no longer alone.

They had been quick to catch up with us, looking like military men experienced in man hunting! The old man had surrounded himself with good, unscrupulous people. The escape continued, and now on that dirt but a wide stretch of road, we would have a better chance of losing them.

‹‹ Come on, gas... they're tailing us! They're getting closer and closer!›› James shouted, hitting me on the shoulder as if I hadn't heard his request.

The first blow was quite mild, and I managed to keep the car still, the second one managed to make me swerve a little, just enough to allow them to pull over to our left and continue ramming us, but I did not refuse the challenge. Suddenly the enemy car re-positioned itself behind us, perhaps they were preparing to give us the coup de grâce. I slammed on the brakes with all the strength I had and nailed the car. Miraculously, we came out almost unharmed, thanks to the seat belts that had held up quite well to that nailing. James was able to protect himself by huddling in the space between the front and back seats, and if he hadn't been so quick on his feet, he would have surely gone through the windshield with his whole body. Two cars blocked our escape route. Four of them got out and, with their guns prominently displayed, they ordered us into their cars. Lorelain was put in the rear car, while James and I were put in the one in front of us. I tried to prevent that division but received a blow in the stomach that caused me a sharp pain, making me bend in two. I could hear Lorelain's screams begging those damned to stop and the boy's moans. He, too, had received his share of punches.

Redemption days

After a short stretch of road, a gate opened in front of us and the cars drove along the avenue until they stopped right in front of the main entrance. The one with my wife, took another destination and I yelled at them to stop and let her free, but it was all wasted breath. The henchmen took us down one by one and accompanied us directly to the boss's study (the same one where Rusty had taken me, before being freed by James), but one of them, the slightly taller one, approached the bookcase and calmly took a book from the third shelf, making a secret passageway appear before our incredulous eyes. The bastards, not only had tied our wrists, but they didn't even deign to tell me where they had taken my wife. The stone stairs descended one floor below the house, and the path was illuminated by neon lamps placed on the ceiling. We went down in the single file, I walked in front of James and the henchmen opened and closed the damn line. I remembered that room, it was the same one I'd been locked up in the first time. The old man hadn't changed the plan, maybe he felt confident it would succeed.

‹‹ Look who came to visit us again. The queer and his little friend››, Rusty, who had the after-effects of his encounter with James on his face, greeted us all smiling and sarcastically addressed us. From the bruises, the boy had come down hard.

‹‹ Free them, while I go and warn him of your arrival: I tell you not to be heroes. The first time was good for you, but it won't be the same for the second time›› and he took the door, followed closely by the armed guards who locked us in.

James wouldn't stop pacing back and forth across the room. He nervously rubbed his hands together, the anticipation of seeing the old man appear short-circuited him. The showdown had come, and we couldn't know how it would turn out; Rusty was right, we weren't going to get away that easily this time. We were just going to have to deal with it.

‹‹ James, stop pacing and sit down. You're making me fucking nervous.››
‹‹ I can't help it... I have to keep walking to keep from going crazy but how the fuck can you be so calm... Lorelain... your wife...››. Her eyes conveyed pure fear, as did the tremor in her voice.
‹‹ Sorry for the reaction, I'm scared too, and not knowing about Lorelain's fate, makes me freak out! Your grandfather is a crazy murderer...››
‹‹ Don't call him that! That bastard is nobody to me! He is a mentally disturbed son of a bitch who has destroyed several lives and should just burn in hell for all the evil he has committed!›› and he unleashed a fist against the bare, cold wall of our prison.
‹‹ You are wrong, nephew. I have a place in heaven, you will burn in the eternal flames of hell as an abomination against nature!››.

At that sentence, we turned around and to our surprise, we saw the bastard in front of the door flanked by his bodyguards, a little further back was his lackey. At that sight, the boy lost all reason and made to hurl himself at him, but I managed to stop him. He was unperturbed and laughed. He enjoyed seeing the desperation and at the same time the fear on our faces. Likewise, he had achieved his goal and he was pleased, but he knew that the game could not be declared closed.

Redemption days

‹‹ Dirty old bastard! What the fuck do you still want from us? Aren't you still happy with what you've done for us?›› James yelled at him with such a rage that the vein on his neck swelled up, and his face turned red.

He didn't make a fuss even on that occasion, so, he motioned to his henchmen to let us sit down. The show had to begin, we had delayed long enough. One of the two hurled himself at the boy and with a lightning move, bent his right arm behind his back, blocking all his attempts to react. He was close to breaking it in two. And calmly he sat him down on a chair. He held back the instinct to scream, so as not to give his tormentor the satisfaction of doing so. Once the big boss took his seat, the two took their places on either side of him, while Rusty remained motionless in front of the door. The chief laughed in amusement, and the satisfaction he felt distorted his face into a grotesque mask.

‹‹ I bring you greetings from your wife. Don't worry, she's fine and safe for the moment››.

I stared him straight in the eye and said, ‹‹ You bastard!›› And he laughed even more.

‹‹ Dear friends, I welcome you back to my modest home, because, on your first visit, you left before the festivities began. Rude behavior››.

James interrupted him with a further outburst of anger and again shouted at him what he thought of him, and to avoid seeing him killed, I laid my hand on his arm, squeezing it tightly. He turned to me with an air of astonishment at that gesture.

‹‹ By the looks of it, the two sweethearts want to be alone to cuddle! Haha!›› and they all laughed in unison. I increased the pressure on his arm, signaling him not to react to the provocation. Eventually, he understood and tried to put on a good face.

‹‹ Let's move on to more serious matters. Did you think you could escape from my mansion and get away with it?›› he said defiantly.

‹‹ We tried, and we almost succeeded,›› I replied in an amused tone.

‹‹ I didn't think you were so funny. Now I suggest you shut up, I hate being interrupted, otherwise, they'll shut you up,›› and the two were not kidding.

‹‹ You know very well that there is a kinship between me and this abomination, so it will not be difficult for you to understand the real reason for my actions.››

Redemption days

Then, he continued addressing the young man: « Our family could not afford to be muddied because of you and your illness, and when you announced your anomaly, you destroyed your parents, and this one in one fell swoop. Fortunately, your father and mother asked for my help in resolving this dramatic situation, so I approached the director of the hospital and arranged for a forced hospitalization within the facility, all at my expense. And how did you thank me? By running away in the middle of treatment with the risk of throwing the family's good name in the mud, you ungrateful nephew! God has always been on my side though, so after you escaped, some trusted associates of mine gave me all the information I needed to hunt you down,» and he let out an evil grin.

« When I learned that you had applied for a training period at his company, I took the ball and set up my revenge. I set the money machine in motion to bribe some of the company's senior executives and the head of human resources to get you accepted into the internship and especially to get you assigned here. Yet another person who let me down. I had big plans for you, you could have had everything I have, instead, you got screwed over by this pansy. You see, they can manipulate the human mind, making what isn't normal appeared normal. And you fell for it like an idiot! Since I couldn't count on you, I opted for another person and so my choice fell on him, and it was you who served him to me on a silver platter! From your look, I understand that you have understood. You're not stupid, but you certainly didn't inherit my genius, because in that case you would have stopped to think about it and you would have understood that the clinic where the one who was fucking you was admitted was the same one where you had been too!».

Arthur! James resisted with stoicism. He was doing violence to hold himself back; his hands, by dint of clenching the armrests, had become red. His veins had swollen, especially the one on his neck, but his face showed no signs of impatience or anger. The contracted muscles made him look like a marble mask. I still held him by the arm, I knew that if he reacted, they would kill him in cold blood to Grandpa's delight.

‹‹ I visited him every weekend to see how he was progressing and, thanks to Dr. Hunter's kind and helpful cooperation, I had the privilege of observing him from behind a special mirror. The work of the doctors was excellent, as was the treatment he was receiving, but unfortunately, the outcome was not what I expected››.
‹‹ Arthur committed suicide because of you, and you killed John and his wife too! You dirty bastard!›› I shouted at him.

Our fits of rage didn't worry him, after all with those armed guards, he felt he was in a barrel of life.

‹‹ The doctors had brainwashed him to transform him into a 'sleeper killer' ready to carry out purifying revenge for the good name of the family, unfortunately, some mistakes were made that thwarted the outcome, as you kindly pointed out to me. But, I certainly won't leave a job half done, it's not my habit.››

Redemption days

Arthur should have committed a murder-suicide with James as the victim. He had arranged everything, including Arthur's false farewell letter, where he explained the reasons for the gesture and everything would have been dismissed as a desperate gesture due to a sentimental breakup. No one would have connected it to them. James couldn't stand listening to that madman any longer. Every admission of guilt corresponded to a jolt in his chair, but he did everything he could to resist. Unfortunately, Arthur's mind gave way during the famous Thanksgiving feast. The love he felt for James and his desire to love clashed furiously against what had been instilled in him during the reprogramming, causing a short circuit that led him to that tragic act. The old man did not worry about those deaths, after all the weakest pawns of the association had been eliminated, strengthening it even more, to his great joy. He interrupted his monologue and started laughing again. His demonic laughter echoed throughout the room in a guttural tone, like the barking of a dying dog.

He laughed. The bastard!

He was laughing at his success! The bastard!

He was laughing at the old bastard!

‹‹ Monster!›› shouted James, getting up from his chair and hurling himself at him. That action displaced everyone and especially the old man, who instantly stopped laughing. I couldn't hold him back, but the old man's gorillas did.

James took a volley of punches in the face that made him fall backward. They both attacked the boy, including Rusty, who hurled himself vehemently and angrily at James while he tried to protect his face and stomach with his hands and arms. In the meantime, the old man had stood up to better observe the scene and at the same time incite them to punch and kick him for the supreme good of the great Aryan American nation. In that confusion, no one paid any attention to yours truly. The nearest guard had his back to me, so he didn't notice the chair coming between his head and neck. He fell to the ground like a big sack of potatoes, screaming in pain from the blow he had received. At that point, the old man incited Rusty to kill me for my insolence.

BANG! BANG!

Two knocks echoed through the room, dropping the surrounding silence. James was still lying on the floor in a fetal position. The old man flattened himself completely against the wall as if that gesture could make him disappear, while the guard froze. Blood was pouring out of two spots on his chest within easy reach of each other, soiling Rusty's clothes, still standing with two bullets in his body, with only a few sideways wobbles that hinted at imminent collapse. His vision was beginning to blur, his breathing was becoming shorter and more labored, and a few trickles of blood could be seen on the sides of his half-open mouth in a grimace of pain. Finally, the legs gave way. The thud of the floor echoed, accompanied by the last gasp of life coming out of his mouth. The last exhalation of a life. Darkness enveloped the entire world. I had killed Rusty.

Redemption days

‹‹ Now I suggest you all take it easy and especially you,›› and I fired two more shots. In the shoulder and leg of one of the henchmen, knocking him off balance. Now the tables were turned.

‹‹ Make yourself look good! I want to see your face, you filthy murderer!›› I ordered the old man, holding him at gunpoint.

‹‹ James, are you all right?›› He nodded, trying to get upright. I couldn't help him, I had to keep an eye on the survivors. The wounded guard had lost consciousness, while the other still lay beside me.

‹‹ Don't think you've won! Abe, you asshole, get up and kill them! I command you... KILL THEM BOTH!››.

I didn't give him time. I fired three more shots from the gun and knocked him out, then took his weapon from its holster. The old man couldn't shut up!

‹‹ Shut up! SHUT UP! SHUT UP!››

James was still staggering slightly, but he was on his feet and staring straight into his eyes, then suddenly he walked up to him and unleashed a barrage of punches. He hit every part of his body. Face. Belly. Lower abdomen. He struck with blind fury and the precision of a skilled boxer. He wasn't sparing himself. Even though he had just taken a beating, the anger, and thirst for revenge gave him the strength to land those punches with power. His shoulders against the wall pinned him down. Blood was pouring out of his mouth and nose, his hands slumped on his hips, and his dull eyes indicated his defeat. I didn't mind that scene at all, but I decided to stop him anyway. The lesson had been more than enough.

‹‹ Enough! Get a grip!›› and I blocked yet another punch. James tried to resist, but then lowered his arm and turned to me. Tears were now running down his face from the tension he had accumulated throughout that time. He hugged me with what little strength he had left inside his exhausted body and whispered a faint 'thank you' in my ear.

‹‹ Let's get out of here. You got your revenge, now it's up to the authorities to finish it. Come on...›› and supporting him for a few steps, we took the way out. Once we got out of that cursed mansion of horrors, we were going to report the old man and his henchmen to the police and I was going to face my fate head-on, whatever it had in store.

That time I wouldn't back down, no... I would pay for the mistakes I had made in the past, but at least the heavy boulder weighing me down had vanished.

‹‹ Where do you think you're going... I'M NOT FINISHED WITH YOU YET!››

BANG! BANG! BANG!

Redemption days

Three sharp, sudden shots echoed through the room again, and this time two out of three-hit me dead on. One bullet lodged on the right side of my chest and the other one tore through my left shoulder blade, making it jump. The pain was excruciating. I closed my eyes and then felt nothing. Many people say that when you are about to die you see your life again like an old black and white film, unfortunately, this was not my case. I didn't even see the famous light at the end of the tunnel, nor did I hear the voices of the many relatives and friends who had died before me, inviting me to go through it, reassuring me that everything would go well and that I shouldn't be afraid, after all, I was going to a better place where there was no suffering and that I would be surrounded by eternal light. Instead of all this, I found myself walking down a long, desolate road with no end in sight, and all around me, desolation, dust, and cold earth. No sign of life, except for myself.

A dark and threatening sky accompanied me on this strange journey. Not even the sun could be seen beyond those strange and unusual dark gray clouds, and the gloom was eerie. The temperature wasn't even supposed to be above 41°F, causing me to shiver and tremble all over my body, and I almost started chattering my teeth. I was wearing a single garment that was both light and ridiculous. It was a simple white gown with a back opening, held closed with laces and that was it. The cold entered me from every little space and, while my bottom was slowly freezing, on the front the process was advanced, and instead of testicles I had two frozen and dried up balls, while my 'tool' was disappearing completely from my sight. My feet, were black and encrusted with all kinds of filth due to the slime that covered the road I was walking on, trying to keep warm, covering my chest with my arms, but it was no use. The gusts of wind were getting stronger and stronger, causing me a slight sense of loss, but I kept walking.

I looked at every part of that extensive landscape, but I could see nothing but nothingness. The road was perfectly straight, without any curves, bumps, or ditches. Smooth, long, flat, and desolate. That's what it looked like to my poor eyes. I turned around once to see where I was coming from and, surprise, it was identical to where I was heading. Maybe it didn't matter which direction I was going, maybe I was going to walk for all eternity looking for the destination I would never reach. If the place I was in was hell, then the hell tourism office hadn't done a very good job!

Redemption days

I got over it, after all, I had committed many crimes in my life, and surely the last actions weren't enough to pay off my debt for good, but they could give me some discount... at most a place in purgatory, right? At that loud question, which no one but me would have heard, I fell to the dusty ground, exhausted and cold in a land not my own, in a time not my own to laugh. A burst of ghostly laughter was gradually turning into a desperate cry. I couldn't stop myself from screaming and crying for my destiny.

A destiny that I had chosen and built for myself action after action during my short life. I remembered the burning and sharp pain in my chest, the flame coming out of the gun, and the cursed smile of the bastard, and that was it. My last memories were of my death.

How ironic! I didn't want to get up, I was tired, and then what would have changed if I had been a few minutes late?

Nothing! At the end of the day I had all eternity to go nowhere, and so in the end sleep took over my poor body, by now exhausted by fatigue and discouragement. The cold became more intense, perhaps because the night was coming (although I doubted that time could exist in that place) and so I settled in the fetal position. I was getting sleepy when I began to hear voices in the distance, faint because of the strong wind blowing. I raised my head, but I put it back safely in my hands. Too cold. I heard those voices again, and this time they were louder.

It sounded like a conversation. A conversation I was witnessing and could not participate in. I didn't understand much of what they were saying, so I decided to get up and head toward those voices. The wind didn't want to drop, on the contrary, it increased with every step I took.

Meanwhile, I followed the sound. I shouted to the voices to keep talking, or rather, I begged them to lead me to my destination. The more I went on, the more the voices increased in intensity, and finally, my steps turned into a light run and then faster and faster. My breath became heavy. The cold air penetrated my lungs, causing me a few painful twinges. I kept running and finally caught a glimpse of light. Maybe I had gotten a free pass to heaven? Possibly.

‹‹ Welcome back to the living, dear!››. That voice was not new to me, that tone could only belong to one person, Lorelain! I slowly opened my eyes, the light outside was too strong, but little by little I got used to it. I could only see the blurred outlines. She was standing in front of me, and she was smiling, even though she must have cried a lot. Her beautiful face was marked by those tears, shed for me.

‹‹ You're alive! You are alive! James...run...he's alive!›› and he pulled me into a hug.

‹‹ You're finally back!›› said James, hugging me with tears in his eyes. Then he pulled away, and I could finally observe my surroundings. I was in a hospital room connected to I don't know how many machines and on my right were James and my wife, on the opposite side a pretty nurse, and in front of my bed stood an old doctor holding my medical records.

Redemption days

‹‹ We had no more hope for his awakening, you know?›› the doctor said, smiling at me as if he had a small child in front of him. I wanted to talk.

I wanted to ask for some explanations about what had happened, but I was prevented, according to them, I was still too weak, and the clinical situation was still uncertain, although I was finally out of danger.

Not only that, but I spent several months in the hospital, and every day both James and Lorelain came to see me, but they both never said anything about the outcome of the crash, carefully avoiding giving me any information.

The day of my discharge from the hospital came. On a warm and sunny day in early summer, they both picked me up and took me home. I felt some pain coming from my shoulder, but it was nothing compared to the pain after waking up. My heart was pounding with excitement and as soon as I crossed the threshold of the apartment a smile escaped me that soon turned into laughter. A liberating laugh. The doctor had prescribed three more weeks of absolute rest, I couldn't exert myself or anything else, soon I would be able to take short walks in the park. Lorelain carried the suitcases into the bedroom and began to put the clothes in the closet (I noticed it was new, she must have bought it to replace the one I had destroyed), while James helped me sit on the lounge chair. I still had some difficulty moving around, but in time I would get back to doing everything myself. Once seated, he asked me: ‹‹ Comfortable? Do you want me to bring you something to drink? To eat? Ask for it››

‹‹ I bet beer doesn't fall under the category of drinking, does it?››

‹‹ True, but we can make it fit anyway. Don't worry, leave it to the genius of the can,››, and turned away to go to the kitchen.

While waiting, I could hear Lorelain humming from the bedroom. A happy and carefree humming that filled my heart with deep joy, and at the same time made me wonder if at least she had recovered from that adventure.

‹‹ Here's your cold beer and one for me too››.

‹‹ Thanks›› I answered taking it in my hands and from the weight of the can I realized that it had been partially emptied by James. There must have been not even three fingers of beer inside. I shook it in front of his eyes to make him understand that I had discovered the trick.

‹‹ Don't make that face, you shouldn't even be drinking any. So don't take it out on that poor guy, you should also thank him for the thought.›› Lorelain intervened.

‹‹ Don't worry, I suspected that, but he could have left at least half of it... couldn't he?››

‹‹ No››.

‹‹ James, instead of sitting there laughing under your breath, could you stand up for me?››.

He shrugged his shoulders, sipped his beer, and patted me on the back as if to say: ‹‹ The game is for two players, not three!››

‹‹ Can I leave you alone without you making trouble?››

‹‹ We're grown-ups but... excuse me Lorelain, how are you?››

Redemption days

‹‹ I'm fine, don't worry. She kissed me. A kiss between two lovers.

‹‹ I'll call you when it's ready. I recommend you be good.›› she said and retreated to the kitchen to prepare one of her excellent lunches. James continued to sneer under his mustache, and I noticed that he was fine.

‹‹ We're on our own now, so tell me whatever you need to tell me. The time is now!›› I told him after watching my wife disappear into the kitchen.

He knew very well what I was referring to and didn't back down, even though he still had doubts about it.

‹‹ Are you sure you want to know the whole story?››

‹‹ Come on James, I want to know the ending. Don't make me beg you. I don't feel like asking Lorelain, I'd feel guilty towards her, you understand me don't you?››

‹‹ I understand your state...damn, I wish I could have delayed the moment of truth any longer.››

‹‹ Speak, I'll be all ears and I promise I won't interrupt you.››

At that point, he began his narration. He started to narrate from the last memories I had, which were the shots fired in the bastard's secret room.

‹‹ The shots were aimed at me, and you saved me by giving me a shoulder bump and making me hit the wall. So you took two bullets while the third one lodged in the wall. I owe you my life, and I can never repay you for that. After you slumped to the ground, I grabbed my gun and returned fire. I don't even know how I did it,›› he froze, unable to continue his story, so I tried to reassure and calm him at the same time.

‹‹ I'm wondering what myself.››

‹‹ I was telling you that they thought you were dead... and I honestly thought so too, and at that point, I fired in his direction. I just grazed him. He fired back and took a glancing blow at me. The aim does not run in my family. Suddenly, just near the entrance of the house, he stopped and decided to face me head-on. A classic duel that only one of us would survive, and I don't need to tell you who won›› He smiled through clenched teeth, a forced but sincere smile. Now and then during the story, I noticed that he looked at a fixed point in the room as if he wanted to avoid looking me straight in the eye.

‹‹ Also in that circumstance that bastard didn't stop talking, but in that case, he did it to answer my questions. I still wanted to know, and he didn't make me beg. I asked him one question, in particular, I wanted to know why he had turned on you. He explained why he had hunted me down, but nothing about his doggedness towards you.››

‹‹ Perhaps it was because I understood his true nature and why I fought him?›› I asked, forgetting my promise not to interrupt him. He did not resent it but was relieved.‹‹ I thought so too at first, but that wasn't the reason.››

‹‹ That wasn't the reason?››

Redemption days

‹‹ That wasn't it, and if you keep interrupting me, it will take me two years to finish the story and for sure, Lorelain will enjoy the delicious meal she is preparing for us all by herself.››

‹‹ OK, kid. Get the hint... you're starving! I'll keep quiet and be good Wolfe promise!››

‹‹ You guessed it, old man!›› and we laughed so heartily and loudly that Lorelain peeked through the kitchen door to check on her two big boys.

‹‹ Are you okay?›› she asked, intrigued by our laughter.

‹‹ Yes, I'm fine. Everything is fine! Your boys are doing very well!›› I replied amused. Assured that everything was going well, she returned to her chores.

In the end, James resumed the story: ‹‹ I was telling you that after having asked him that question, he stopped suddenly and pronounced some incomprehensible phrase. At that point, I took advantage and shot him in the shoulder before he did. He screamed in pain, dropped the gun, and with that hand tried to stop the blood from spilling, then he fell to the ground. I swear to you... my hand was shaking so much from the accumulated fear that even my gun slipped out of my hands... man what an experience... what a damn experience... I walked over to him, I don't know exactly why I did that, and knelt by his side... and... and... damn!››.

He got up from the chair and, putting his hands in his hair in a desperate and convulsive gesture, he went back and forth in the hall and then stopped in front of me: «‹ I called him by name, and I held him in my arms. He made no resistance to my contact, he didn't have the strength, the wound was deep and serious... and he felt that the end was near. I asked him that question again and as an answer, I only got sibylline and incomprehensible sentences. The only comprehensible ones were these: Klaus and he knows it... letters... the letters... and before he expired: 'You and me, we are more alike than you think. Unfortunately, the bullet had punctured his lung badly, and the rescuers could not get there in time to save him. Curious though... you took two bullets and saved yourself, he only took one and died. Life happens. Help and the police arrived. Lorelain had managed to call the police through her smartphone. The two guys had abandoned her as soon as they heard the shots. You lost a lot of blood, but they managed to save you, unfortunately, you remained in a coma for several weeks, the doctors told us that there was a risk that you wouldn't make it but, since you are here in front of me, they were wrong. During the trial, all the acts of the association came to light, it was declared illegal and some of their members were arrested and convicted of hate crimes. For my part, I got off with a "no contest"; after all, it was self-defense, which was also invoked in your case. As for my beating... well... I didn't say anything. No one connected that episode to the association or you. Sometimes you have to be able to forgive and forget. We had already suffered enough, and it would have been useless for you to spend the rest of your life behind bars. You saved my life and certain actions should not be forgotten.››.

Redemption days

He had calmed down, and I was surprised by his gesture of humanity toward me. He had shown himself to be a boy with a heart of gold. I could have said any phrase of thanks, but I didn't, sometimes silence is worth a thousand words.

‹‹ Do those sentences tell you anything? Did they make you turn on that famous light bulb?››

‹‹ Nothing. Complete darkness. And to you?››

‹‹ Nothing... maybe...››

‹‹ Maybe what?››

‹‹ Perhaps when he said that he and I were alike, he was referring to our family connection...››

‹‹ Sure, he was referring to the family bond and maybe deep down he loved you.››

‹‹ A strange way to prove his love to me. Strange. Let's go and eat, lunch is ready... come on, I'll help you up, come on old man.››

‹‹ Before long, this so-called old man will beat you at basketball with one hand tied behind his back, you can be sure of that!›› and I laughed with amusement.

The table and the lunch were those of the great occasions, all excellent. During the meal, we talked about the news that I had missed during my comatose state, so I learned that James was dating a boy, or rather, as my wife said: "a doctor".

The story was just beginning, and she didn't know how it would develop, but she was enjoying every moment with him. At that point, I suggested that we bring him home for dinner to get to know him, and both he and Lorelain were enthusiastic about the invitation. At that point, I realized that something inside me had changed. Changed for the better... and I smiled at that change. Lunch continued most pleasantly. I had found my wife's love and the warmth of a son.

Several months passed, and during that time I was reborn. The divorce was annulled, and we renewed our promise of marriage with a small private ceremony our witnesses were James and Michael. Their relationship was consolidated, and between the ups and downs typical of any romantic relationship, they had decided to take the big step of living together, and then came the day of the wedding. As soon as Lorelain heard the news, she immediately started to organize the event in detail. They were the worst two weeks of my life. That woman seemed to be tireless and managed to extricate herself by cleverly solving every problem that arose, and the best part was that she managed to put me in the middle of that adventure. James asked us to be his witnesses, in particular, he asked Lorelain to walk him down the aisle, a request that made her burst with joy. A simple and sober ceremony. The wedding was officiated in the municipality, then followed the reception in the inn of Mrs. Olmert, (Now, when we needed to escape from the hectic city life, that place was ideal for rest and, after so long, it seemed to be hosted by distant relatives). After the damage done to Lorelain's family cabin, my in-laws forbade us to set foot there.

Redemption days

It was a day I will never forget. Dancing, laughter, wine, and lots of normalcy.

Work was going pretty well, I had also stopped drinking and was keeping fit by going to the gym, something I never thought I would be able to do, but towards the end of the year, we were told incredible news. We were expecting a baby! Lorelain was pregnant, and I can only say that this news changed our lives even more. Her wish was taking shape, and perhaps mine as well. As soon as we found out the sex of the new baby, we started stocking up on all kinds of baby items. We changed our house to one in the suburbs with a small garden, so our baby would have plenty of room to play outside. We joked that James was going to have a baby sister, but underneath it was the truth. James was now more than just a friend or co-worker, he was something more. A son.

A month after little Lucy was born, I found myself alone at home. Lorelain had brought the child to her parents, James and Michael had taken advantage of a few days off to take a trip to Paris, a sort of honeymoon, so I devoted myself to reading. I was reading letters, years old. Letters are written in German, of which I had lost the memory. My German was no longer what it used to be, but I understood the meaning very well. I read them one after the other. As soon as I finished reading one, I moved on to the next, and every thought I read made me better understand the whole story. A story with sad, bleak, and dramatic developments. And that if he had taken another direction, perhaps there would not have been all that bloodshed of which I had become an accomplice, despite myself.

Epilogue

Redemption days

The epistolary was about Klaus and Helmut, longtime friends in post-war Germany. By the end of the reading, the fog finally cleared from my mind and the whole story took shape. A tragic and at the same time moving story. Helmut, who was just ten years old at the end of the Second World War and the collapse of the Nazi regime, was part of the young recruits who defended the capital house to house from the advance of the Red Army. He had a youth card of the Nazi Party in his pocket, as did all members of his family, and blindly believed in the delusional theories that had been inculcated since his birth by the Third Reich and its supreme leader. Even after the fall, he never stopped believing in them. The post-war period was terrible, including poverty and the premature loss of his father and older brother on the Russian front, so in him matured the idea that only good resided in that doctrine. Once he grew up he clandestinely joined the various associations that were based on Nazism, and he always showed his determination and his loyalty to those ideals. The meeting with Klaus took place in front of the Berlin State University, while Helmut and his comrades were spreading leaflets to look for recruits for their movement. From what I understood, their first meeting was quite stormy, in fact, from the exchange of insults for different political views, it turned into facts. The fight spread to other people and was quelled only by the arrival of the police, and Helmut swore revenge against the person who had dared to stand up to him. When he managed to get all the information about his rival, he spent days following him to understand his habits and hit him when he least expected that day did not take long to arrive but the story did not go as he imagined it. One night Klaus was returning home after a day spent with his friends, and lost a few minutes to find the keys to the house, when he was shot in the back of the head and fell unconscious in front of the door of his building, waking up a few minutes later tied to a chair in a room unknown to him. He understood that he had been kidnapped, and he also knew by whom. Helmut presented himself as a member of an imaginary political party for the rebirth of the Fourth Reich and accused him of high treason against the Aryan Nation and from that moment they began to argue. Slaps flew as well, but the acts of physical violence were limited to that. There were only the two of them in the room. The demonstrative action was organized and carried out only by him, he didn't ask for help from any of his comrades the matter had to be solved between them and that was it. It was a personal matter. In the letters, it was not clearly stated, but at a certain point, so without explaining, she untied him, and they stayed talking all night as if they were longtime friends. They parted at the first rays of dawn, Klaus took a bus to go back, but he left that house with a changed soul, and Helmut too had undergone a change that would take place only a few months later. The two of them went back to their usual lives, until the day Helmut apologized to Klaus for his behavior and invited him to a picnic to make up for what had happened. He had no hesitation whatsoever, he didn't even think of a trap, after all, he trusted him.

It was enough to read a passage from a letter from Klaus in which he recalled the event that would change the lives of many people.

Redemption days

"My memories are still sharp, even after all these months. How could I forget that wonderful afternoon spent in your company? I couldn't and neither could you, and you know it better than I do. The endless discussions, your nervousness in looking me straight in the eye as you spoke to me, made you look like a helpless puppy trying to explore the new world in front of him with curiosity mixed with fear of novelty. We sat in the grass, side by side talking and your hand wouldn't stop moving on my thigh... until the moment when I put mine on it. You became as still as a marble statue. You didn't expect it, but I'm sure that in your heart, you wanted it to happen. Not only that, but you looked up at me, and after a long time I could see the icy blue in your eyes that emanated an intensity and a warmth of soul that warmed my heart. You put your lips to mine and we both knew that our lives would be joined, like our bodies".

He couldn't accept himself.

He could not be a sexual abomination, one of those who had to be locked up in concentration camps, those he considered inferior. He could not be.

He wasn't.

He was part of the chosen race that would rule the world. That was his destiny, and he had always known it.

He finally concluded that he had been led astray by that abnormal.

A trap to weaken the organization, yes... a trap... a trap! He decided to confront him and put an end to the whole thing and prevent the word from spreading. No, he couldn't let that happen! At that point, he confronted him head-on and beat the crap out of him. He unloaded all his frustrations on him, blow after blow, raging on his beloved, the person who represented that impure and unworthy love! Klaus cashed in without reacting. He let himself be insulted and beaten. In the end, he left him examined, covered in blood and bruises, his clothes torn, and he ran away. From that day on, they never saw each other again. Helmut put his mind at rest and went on with his life, trying to make it as normal as possible. Now the danger of a leak had been averted, after that lesson the coward would not have dared to open his mouth, otherwise, he would have sought him out to close the matter definitively. With his death! He got engaged to a girl and after not even three months he decided to impale her. The preparations were made in a hurry. Only a few intimates were invited, no outsiders were to disturb the ceremony. He also put up a kind of cordon of protection, to avoid unpleasant surprises. The newlyweds changed cities and moved several miles away from their birthplace, but after not even a year a letter arrived. An unexpected and dreaded letter that came from the past.

Redemption days

"Dear Helmut, many heartfelt congratulations on your marriage. During our last meeting, you remember it well, don't you? Yes, you do... I couldn't tell you something important, because you wouldn't let me speak. Your fists and insults spoke. At that moment, you had to take it out on someone to clear your conscience and hide your true self from the eyes of the world. I saw you at your wedding, quiet I kept my distance from your ridiculous security cordon, but I could see you well... your eyes, once warm, full of love and vitality had lost their best side. I saw them only icy and cold, full of hate and devoid of any feeling. Running away from yourself will get you nowhere. You will keep running, and wherever you go in the world, you will never find a safe place, you will always have to confront your true soul. Eventually, you will have to face yourself! How I felt about you has not changed. You will always be in my thoughts. Your Klaus."

Reading those writings, one could well understand their state of mind. I cannot explain why he had decided to keep all the letters, he could have made them disappear forever by feeding them to the fire, but he did not. He had kept them jealously for all those years, and I'm sure now and then Helmut found himself alone reading them and thinking about the past. He escaped further and moved across the ocean. To the United States. And there he felt safe, but it was short-lived. He could not escape from himself, he had understood. His wife gave him two beautiful heirs, and he devoted himself again to politics. He founded his association to fight his battle against all those he considered harmful to the new rebirth of the Aryan race in the United States. He even changed his first and last names and Americanized them after receiving American citizenship.

A new life. A new nation. A new identity. But an old soul.

Klaus stayed behind to live in Germany. He was not running away from himself. He had understood his true self and accepted it; after all, there was nothing abnormal about it. The love he felt for his partner had nothing different or inferior or insane compared to a so-called straight love. He lived it out in the open and continued to live it even with all the mistrust, hatred, and bigotry of thought that surrounded him and the hostility from his family. He fought his battle, along with everyone else, to shout to the world that love has only one meaning: to LOVE! Having no children, she left her few possessions to the Human Rights Association, but would never know that she had unwittingly altered the course of her only grandchild's life. An unknown nephew in her eyes. An unknown uncle in his nephew's eyes. A nephew who had taken a wrong turn that was leading him into an abyss of loneliness and resentment and fear of the unknown.

At this point... I thank you from the bottom of my heart, dear Uncle Klaus. A loving hug from your nephew.

Redemption days

Published

2019 2020 2021 **2022** 2023 2024

○